KT-210-332

JOHN CONSTANTINE, HELLBLAZER: H I G H W A T E R

JOHN CONSTANTINE, HELLBLAZER:
# HIGHWATER

Brian Azzarello
Writer

Marcelo Frusin
Giuseppe Camuncoli
Cameron Stewart
Artists

Lee Loughridge
James Sinclair
Colorists

Clem Robins
Letterer

Tim Bradstreet
Original Series Covers

| | |
|---|---|
| Karen Berger | VP-Executive Editor |
| Will Dennis, Tony Bedard | Editors-original series |
| Zachary Rau, Tammy Beatty | Assistant Editors-original series |
| Scott Nybakken | Editor-collected edition |
| Robbin Brosterman | Senior Art Director |
| Paul Levitz | President & Publisher |
| Georg Brewer | VP-Design & Retail Product Development |
| Richard Bruning | Senior VP-Creative Director |
| Patrick Caldon | Senior VP-Finance & Operations |
| Chris Caramalis | VP-Finance |
| Terri Cunningham | VP-Managing Editor |
| Dan DiDio | VP-Editorial |
| Alison Gill | VP-Manufacturing |
| Rich Johnson | VP-Book Trade Sales |
| Hank Kanalz | VP-General Manager-WildStorm |
| Lillian Laserson | Senior VP & General Counsel |
| Jim Lee | Editorial Director-WildStorm |
| David McKillips | VP-Advertising & Custom Publishing |
| John Nee | VP-Business Development |
| Gregory Noveck | Senior VP-Creative Affairs |
| Cheryl Rubin | VP-Brand Management |
| Bob Wayne | VP-Sales & Marketing |

**JOHN CONSTANTINE, HELLBLAZER: HIGHWATER**

Published by DC Comics. Cover and compilation copyright © 2004 DC Comics. All Rights Reserved.

Originally published in single magazine form as HELLBLAZER 164-174. Copyright © 2001, 2002 DC Comics. All Rights Reserved. All characters, their distinctive likenesses and related elements featured in this publication are trademarks of DC Comics. The stories, characters and incidents featured in this publication are entirely fictional. DC Comics does not read or accept unsolicited submissions of ideas, stories or artwork.

DC Comics, 1700 Broadway, New York, NY 10019
A Warner Bros. Entertainment Company
Printed in Canada. First Printing.

ISBN: 1-4012-0223-3

Cover illustration by Tim Bradstreet.

Publication design by Peter Hamboussi.

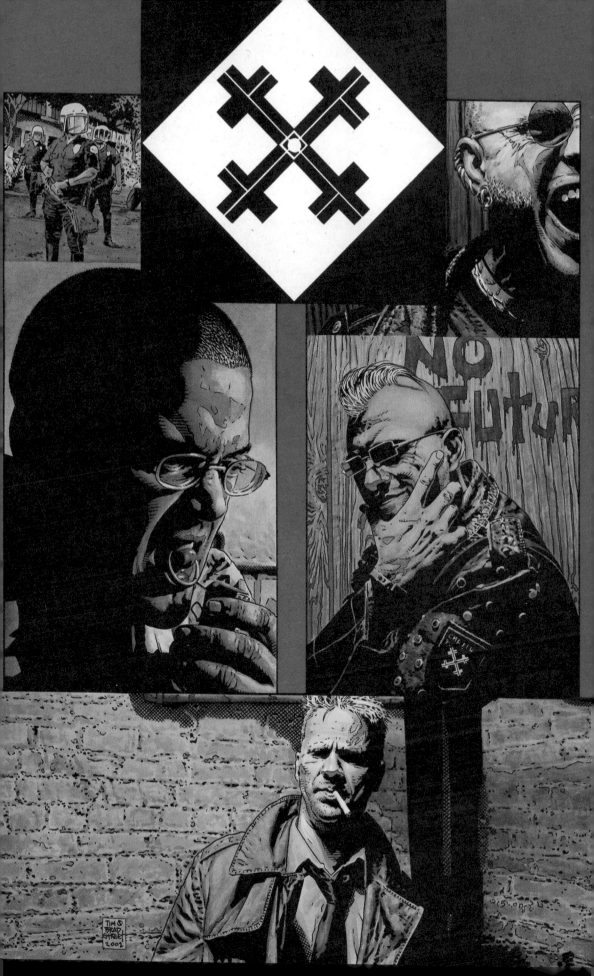

"GOD BREATHED LIFE INTO *ADAM*.

"MEANING HE GAVE HIM A DIVINE SPIRIT, WHICH *SEPARATED* HIM FROM ALL CREATION.

"MEANING HE WAS *SPECIAL* TO GOD.

"THE NAME *ADAM* MEANS 'TO SHOW BLOOD IN THE FACE.'

"MEANING HE COULD *BLUSH*.

"MEANING HE WAS *WHITE*."

"AND GOD GAVE ADAM *DIVINITY* OVER THE GARDEN, AND BROUGHT ALL THE 'BEASTS OF THE FIELD' BEFORE HIM, SO HE COULD CHOOSE A 'HELP MATE.'

"MEANING A *WIFE.*

"MEANING THESE *BEASTS,* THEY HAD TO HAVE *HUMAN* FORM.

"BUT ADAM FOUND NO SUITABLE WIFE AMONG THEM, SO GOD TOOK A *RIB* FROM ADAM...

"...MEANING A PIECE CLOSE TO HIS *HEART...*

"...AND USED IT TO CREATE *EVE.*

"MEANING HER *PURPOSE* WAS TO ESTABLISH A *WHITE RACE,* A NOBLE RACE, DEARER TO GOD THAN ALL THE *OTHER* RACES ON THE FACE OF HIS EARTH."

"BUT EVE, SHE WAS TEMPTED BY *SATAN*, IN HUMAN-LIKE FORM--NOT AS A *SNAKE*...

"...BUT AS A *PENIS*.

"MEANING SHE LAID DOWN WITH A MAN *OTHER* THAN ADAM.

"MEANING THE FALL FROM GRACE WAS NOT ONLY *SEXUAL* IN NATURE.

"AND ADAM, *HE* PARTOOK IN THE FRUIT AS WELL, AS IT WAS 'PLEASANT TO THE EYES' AND CAPABLE OF MAKING MEN WISE.

"BUT THIS *EARTHLY* KNOWLEDGE, THE COST WAS *HIGH*, AND THE KNOWING *PAINFUL*."

CHEERS.

SAY SQUIRE, WAS WONDERIN' IF YOU COULD *HELP* ME.

WHAT MAKES YOU THINK I *CAN*?

WELL, I FOUND IF I *NEED* SOMETHING, USUALLY A BLOKE ON THAT SIDE A THE BAR CAN *GIVE* IT TO ME.

I'M LOOKING FOR THIS BIRD --MARJORIE FERMIN? Y'KNOW HER?

DO I KNOW YOU?

NO.

RIGHT.

JIMMY!

POO

FE BEER

WHY YA LOOKIN' FOR *MARJORIE* FOR?

I WAS MATES WITH HER *HUSBAND*.

War Skin

HE GOT *KILLED*, DIDN'T HE?

S'RIGHT, AN' I GOT PUT IN PRISON FOR *DOIN'* IT.

"MEANING THAT IN THE ACT OF ORIGINAL SIN, THE *SATANIC RACE* WAS BORN.

"MEANING THAT EVE HAD CONCEIVED A CHILD OF *SATAN* AS WELL AS *ADAM.* CAIN AND ABEL--TWIN SONS OF DIFFERENT FATHERS.

"MEANING ONLY *ABEL* CARRIED ADAM'S BLOODLINE, WHICH WAS RIGHTEOUS AND PURE.

"AND CAIN, HE COULD FIND *NO FAVOR* WITH GOD.

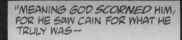

"MEANING GOD *SCORNED* HIM, FOR HE SAW CAIN FOR WHAT HE TRULY WAS--

"--A *MONGREL.*"

"SO IN THE FIRST ACT OF JEALOUSY, CAIN *MURDERED* ABEL, SPILLING HIS PURE BLOOD, AND GOD CAST CAIN *OUT* OF THE GARDEN..."

"...MEANING HE WAS FORCED TO ROAM THE LAND--

"--AND HE WAS BEARING A *MARK*...

"...MEANING THAT HE WAS *PHYSICALLY DIFFERENT*.

MAIL
726

"MEANING HE WAS THE FIRST *JEW*."

THE BIBLE

DISGUISED? 'FRAID *NOT*, SUN-SHINE. THE SO-CALLED *GOSPEL TRUTH* IS WIDE FUCKIN' OPEN TO *INTER-PRETATION*, MEAN-ING EVERY GIT--

--AN' THEY ARE *LEGION*--

--THAT PUTS ANY *CREDENCE* IN THE *GOOD BOOK* CAN LOOK TO IT AS *DIVINE JUSTIFICATION* FOR THEIR BLOODY EARTHBOUND AGENDAS.

HE'S FUCKIN' *NUTJOB*, eh?

WHAT DO YOU THINK HE'S *DOIN'*?

I DUNNO... MAYBE HE'S *REHEARSIN'* WHAT HE'S GOT TO SAY TO *MARJORIE*.

*LOSER.*

"THE PURE WHITE BLOODLINE OF ADAM WAS DEAR TO GOD."

"BUT AS THEY GREW IN NUMBER, AGAIN AND AGAIN *THE SIN OF EVE* WAS COMMITTED.

"MEANING THE RACE WAS FURTHER *MONGRELIZED.*

"MEANING THEY *VIOLATED* GOD'S LAW.

"AND THIS *ANGERED* GOD, FOR HE HAD CREATED THE WHITE RACE TO BE *SPECIAL* TO HIM, NOT TO BE SWALLOWED UP AND *POLLUTED* THROUGH INTERMARRIAGE WITH THE *DARKER* RACES.

"SO GOD INSTRUCTED *NOAH,* 'A *JUST* MAN PURE IN HIS GENERATIONS'...

"...MEANING *RACIALLY PURE*--

"--TO BUILD AN ARK."

"AND GOD *FLOODED* THE LANDS HELD BY THE SINNERS AND THEIR MONGREL OFFSPRING.

"MEANING HE *CLEANSED* THE EARTH OF ALL THAT OFFENDED HIS EYE.

"WHEN THE FLOOD HAD SUBSIDED, GOD THEN TOLD NOAH, AND HIS WIFE, AND THEIR CHILDREN, 'BE FRUITFUL, AND MULTIPLY.'

"MEANING *POPULATE* THE WORLD, RESTORING THE RACIAL PURITY AND THE INTEGRITY OF THE *WHITE RACE*..."

"HE GAVE THEM STRENGTH, AND A STRAIGHTNESS OF CHARACTER, FOR HE LOVED THEM MORE THAN ALL HIS CREATION.

"MEANING THAT HE HAD CREATED EVERYTHING FOR *THEM*.

"THEY WERE TO *CONQUER* THE WILDERNESS...

"...*MULTIPLY* INTO GREAT NUMBERS...

"...AND *SETTLE* IN A LAND PROMISED TO THEM.

"A BEAUTIFUL, *BOUNTIFUL* LAND OF GREAT AGRICULTURAL AND MINERAL WEALTH.

"MEANING THE *GREATEST NATION* ON EARTH..."

...MEANING AMERICA.

I'M VERY PROUD OF YOU, YOU KNOW THAT?

TELL ME, GWYNNETH, WHAT HAPPENED TO OUR PROMISED LAND?

IT WAS TAKEN FROM US IN EIGHTEEN SIXTY-FIVE.

THAT'S RIGHT. BY THE MOST EVIL, MOST VILE, MOST CORRUPT GOVERN-MENT ON THE FACE OF THE EARTH...

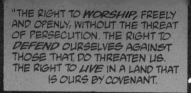

"THE RIGHT TO *WORSHIP*, FREELY AND OPENLY, WITHOUT THE THREAT OF PERSECUTION. THE RIGHT TO *DEFEND* OURSELVES AGAINST THOSE THAT, DO THREATEN US. THE RIGHT TO *LIVE* IN A LAND THAT IS OURS BY COVENANT.

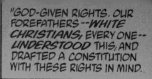

"GOD-GIVEN RIGHTS. OUR FOREFATHERS--*WHITE CHRISTIANS*, EVERY ONE-- *UNDERSTOOD* THIS, AND DRAFTED A CONSTITUTION WITH THESE RIGHTS IN MIND.

"THEREFORE, THE CONSTITUTION IS A POLITICAL *AND* A *CHRISTIAN* DOCUMENT THAT EXPLAINS BOTH OUR *RIGHTS*...

"...AND OUR *OBLIGATIONS*. THERE IS *NO* SEPARATION OF CHURCH AND STATE, AS THE ENEMY WOULD HAVE YOU BELIEVE."

"THESE ARE ACTS OF *WAR*."

# HIGHWATER

## PART TWO OF FOUR

BRIAN
**AZZARELLO**
writer

MARCELO
**FRUSIN**
artist

CLEM
**ROBINS**
letterer

JAMES
**SINCLAIR**
colorist

**ZYLONOL**
separator

TIM
**BRADSTREET**
cover

TAMMY
**BEATTY**
asst. editor

TONY
**BEDARD**
editor

"...I KNEW BLOODY WELL WHAT HE WAS GONNA DO WITH IT."

LUCKY SET YOU UP, JOHN.

YOU GOT LOCKED UP FOR HIS MURDER.

DOESN'T THAT BOTHER YOU?

TRUTH BE TOLD, NO.

S'FUNNY, YA SNUFF YOURSELF, THEY CALL YA A VICTIM OF SUICIDE.

BOLLOCKS.

THE REAL VICTIMS ARE THE LIVING-- YOUR BLOODY LOVED ONES-- LEFT BEHIND TO QUESTION, IF THERE WAS SOMETHING --ANYTHING-- THEY COULD 'AVE DONE TO PREVENT IT.

YOU THINK I'M A VICTIM, JOHN?

I WENT TO PRISON SO YOU WOULDN'T THINK YOU WERE.

"A WAR BEING WAGED BY THE GOVERNMENT OF THE UNITED STATES AGAINST THE *CITIZENS OF AMERICA.*

"A MOST EVIL AND CORRUPT WAR *IMAGINABLE.*

"A SATANIC WAR.

"WHICH MEANS THOSE WHO DEFEND OUR RIGHTS, *PATRIOTIC MEN* JUST AS BRAVE AS OUR REVOLUTIONARY *ANCESTORS,* FIGHT A *HOLY WAR.*"

"AND THESE WARRIORS ARE LEADERLESS, BY NECESSITY. THEY ARE ALL AROUND, BUT NOWHERE.

"THEY HAVE NO HEAD-QUARTERS, NO MEETING HALLS, NO STOREFRONTS.

"THEY HAVE NO VOICE IN THE JEW-CONTROLLED MEDIA, NO MAGAZINES, NO RADIO, NO TV.

"BUT THEY ARE EVERYWHERE...

"...THEY ARE A LIFE FORCE."

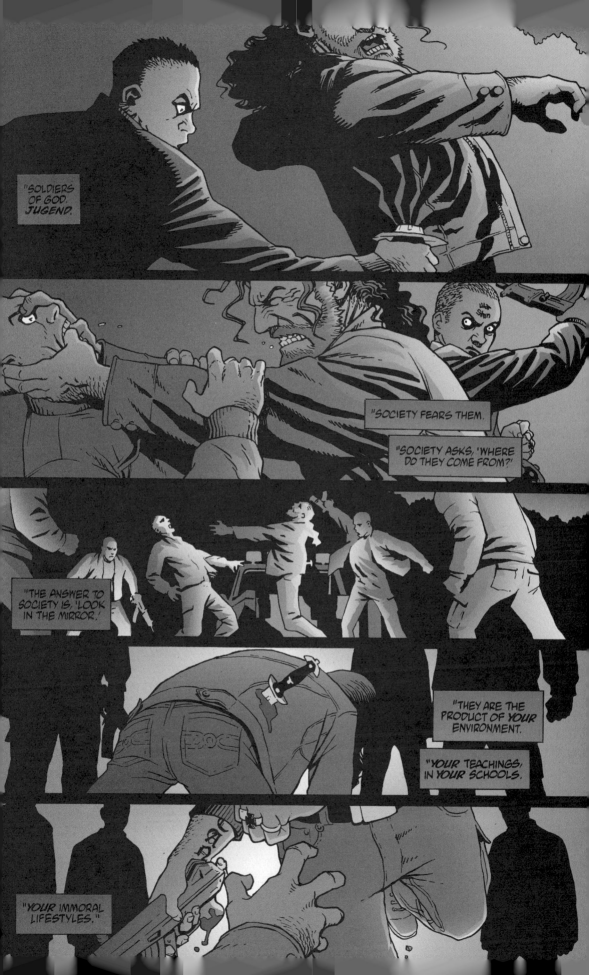

"SOLDIERS OF GOD. JUGEND.

"SOCIETY FEARS THEM.

"SOCIETY ASKS, 'WHERE DO THEY COME FROM?'

"THE ANSWER TO SOCIETY IS, 'LOOK IN THE MIRROR.'

"THEY ARE THE PRODUCT OF YOUR ENVIRONMENT.

"YOUR TEACHINGS, IN YOUR SCHOOLS.

"YOUR IMMORAL LIFESTYLES."

"THEY UNDERSTAND WHAT [THIS] COUNTRY HAS *BECOME*. [THEY] SEE THE EVIL THAT YOU'VE INFLICTED ON THEM AND O[N] THE ENTIRE WHITE RACE.[.]

"WITH YOUR INTEGRATION.

"WITH YOUR AFFIRMATIVE ACTION.

"WITH YOUR SINFUL TOLERA[NCE] FOR EVERY FILTHY PERVERS[ION] AND VULGAR CORRUPTION [THAT] FILLS THEIR HEARTS WITH *RIGHTEOUS ANGE[R]*.

"THEY HAVE *REJECTED* YOU AND ALL YOU *STAND* FOR.

"YOU'VE TURNED FROM *GOD* AND THEY'VE TURNED FROM *YOU*..."

YOU WERE *WRONG* IN BRINGING HIM HERE, MARJORIE.

YOU SHOULD GO NOW.

YOU MISUNDERSTAND ME, MAJOR GAGE.

WHAT YOU'VE SAID--

IT MAKES SENSE...

...AN' THAT...

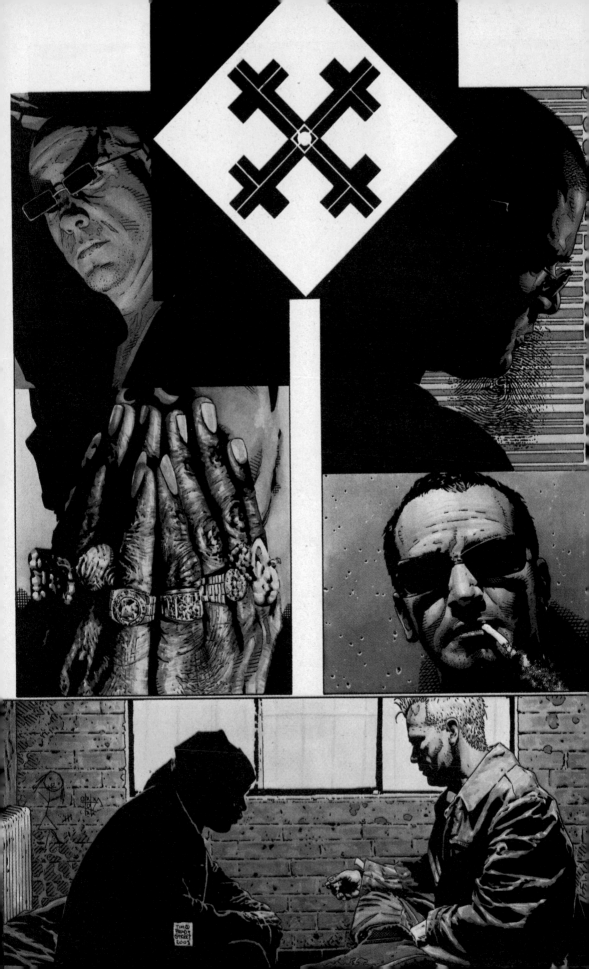

"HATRED IS DESTRUCTIVE.

"IF YOU *HATE* SOMETHING, YOU WANT TO *TEAR* IT DOWN, *RIP* IT APART.

"MAKE IT *WORTHLESS*.

"I HATED MYSELF FOR MORE YEARS THAN I CARE TO REMEMBER."

"ALL MY LIFE, I FELT... *INADEQUATE*. LIKE WHO I WAS, WASN'T ENOUGH...

"...AND WHAT I WAS, WASN'T *RIGHT*.

"NOT JUST HOLDING THE SHORT STICK, BUT *BEING* THE SHORT STICK.

"I COULDN'T EVER MEASURE UP TO WHAT I SAW I WAS SUPPOSED TO.

"*NOT* THE PEOPLE ON THE TV...

"...OR IN MAGAZINES...

"...OR IN THE MOVIES. I COULD *NEVER* BE THAT WAY. I'D *NEVER* LOOK THAT *GOOD*, OR LIVE IN A HOUSE THAT *BIG*, OR HAVE THAT KIND OF *MONEY* OR THAT KIND OF *LOVE*.

"NEVER EVER."

# HIGHWATER

## PART THREE OF FOUR

BRIAN
**AZZARELLO**
writer

MARCELO
**FRUSIN**
artist

JAMES
**SINCLAIR**
colorist

CLEM
**ROBINS**
letterer

**ZYLONOL**
separator

TIM
**BRADSTREET**
cover

WILL
**DENNIS**
editor

B-DEEP
B-DEEP

B-DEEP
B-DEEP

ADOLPH'S BUTCHER SHOP.

YOU MIND TELLING ME WHERE THE FUCK YOU ARE?

HMM. I'D SAY I'M UP TO ME ELBOWS IN IT.

WOLFMAN?

THAS' THIS SAD BLOKE'S NAME?

CLICK

MR. MANOR?

KNOK KNOK

COME IN, FREDO.

SIR, I JUST TRIED CALLING WOLFMAN...

"I FELT ASHAMED."

"ASHAMED, BECAUSE I WAS TAUGHT A LIE-- A MYTH.

"AMERICA. 'LAND OF THE FREE, HOME OF THE BRAVE.' WISHFUL THINKING.

"SELF-DECEPTION.

"... BUT NOT SELF-INFLICTED--WE'RE PROGRAMMED FROM THE TIME WE CAN BARELY READ TO BELIEVE THIS AS FACT.

"A MYTH-- LIBERTY AND PERSONAL FREEDOM.

"IF WE'RE SO FREE, WHY ARE WE SO ENSLAVED TO LICENSES, RESTRICTIONS, PERMITS-- TAXES--THAT OUR FREE-DOMS EXIST SOLELY ON THE WHIMS OF THE GOVERN-MENT?

"FREEDOM'S A MYTH."

"'ALL MEN ARE CREATED EQUAL.' WE'RE TAUGHT THIS *MYTH* TOO, WHEN IT'S SUCH AN OBVIOUS FACT TO BOTH WHITES *AND BLACKS...*

"...THAT IT'S *JUST NOT TRUE.*

"IF WE'RE SO *EQUAL,* WHY DO WE NEED *REVERSE DISCRIMINATION?* AFFIRMATIVE ACTION, QUOTA SYSTEMS --WELFARE?

"IT DOESN'T EVEN SEEM LIKE THE LIBERALS THAT *CAME UP WITH* THESE POLICIES *BELIEVE* BLACKS ARE EQUAL.

"AND THEY *DON'T.* THE TRUTH IS--THIS COUNTRY'S GONE TO THE *DEVIL.*

"AND THE PEOPLE THAT ARE *DESTROYING* WHAT WAS ONCE GREAT ABOUT IT AND TEACHING US TO *HATE* OURSELVES THROUGH THEIR *MEDIA* ARE ONE AND THE SAME..."

...THE JEWS.

I MEAN, NO ONE SCREAMS "EQUALITY" *LOUDER* THAN THE JEWS.

AND NO ONE BELIEVES IT *LESS*.

'CEPT *YOU*.

SO MARJORIE, WHO YOU HATE MORE, THE *JEWS* OR THE *BLACKS*?

JOHN, IT'S NOT ABOUT HATRED OF OTHER RACES, BUT LOVE OF ONE'S OWN.

AND MY RACIAL BELIEFS ARE BASED ON SCRIPTURAL TEACHINGS.

TAUGHT BY *WHO*?

ELLISON GAGE POINTED ME IN THE RIGHT DIRECTION. THE TEACHINGS ARE IN THE *BIBLE*.

WRITTEN IN *BLACK* AN' *WHITE*, I S'POSE.

LOOK, FOR ME TO DECIDE JUST ON MY OWN THAT ANOTHER RACE IS INFERIOR WITH NO SCRIPTURAL BASIS FOR THAT DECISION WOULD BE *SINFUL*.

AND LIKE IT OR NOT, GOD CREATED THE *BLACKS*, JUST AS HE DID *CATS* AND *DOGS*. AND HATING ANY OF GOD'S CREATIONS IS MORALLY *WRONG*.

BUT *GOD* DIDN'T CREATE THE JEWS--*SATAN* DID. AND THEY WON'T REST UNTIL ME AND THE PEOPLE LIKE ME EITHER TURN THEIR BACKS TO GOD OR ARE WIPED FROM THE FACE OF CREATION.

AND DON'T THINK FOR A SECOND THEY HAVEN'T ALREADY STARTED. IN THIS COUNTRY NOW, I'M SUPPOSED TO FEEL *ASHAMED* FOR BEING AN *AMERICAN* AND A *CHRISTIAN.*

I *HATE* THOSE *RESPONSIBLE* FOR THAT--THE *JEWS.* THE CHILDREN OF SATAN.

THANKS FOR CLEARIN' THAT BIT UP. BUT SOMETHIN'... IT DON' SEEM...

...KOSHER.

IF IT'S *WRONG* TO HATE ANY OF THE GOOD LORD'S CREATIONS...

--I BELIEVE IT'S A *SIN.*

RIGHT, RIGHT. A *SIN.* SO TELL ME THEN...

...WHO *CREATED* SATAN?

NIGHT.

69

'OW 'BOUT A PINT, THEN?

HEH. LOOKS LIKE THE *MAJOR'S* BEEN 'ROUND.

YOU SONOFA--

--NOW NOW, LADS, LET'S MIND OUR TONGUES...

...SEEIN' WE'S ALL IN ON THE SAME *SECRET*.

70

BULLSHIT!

WE'RE *BEHIND* THE MAJOR, WE BELIEVE IN HIM, WHEN THE *SHIT* HITS--HE CAN *COUNT* ON US.

'COURSE WE CAN, LADS, 'COURSE WE CAN...

...AN' I'LL MAKE *CERTAIN* HE KNOWS AS MUCH, *LEAVE IT TA ME.*

SEE, I THINK WE MIGHT BE BETTER SERVED...

...SENDING *ANOTHER* MESSAGE.

DON' YOU?

HEY.

YOU LOOKIN' TO BREAK INTA SOMETHIN'?

BREAK IN? NO NEED FOR THAT...

...THE DOOR'S WIDE FUCKING OPEN.

"I BELIEVE IF YOU DON'T *LIVE* FOR *SOMETHING*, YOU'LL *DIE* FOR NOTHING.

"I BELIEVE I LIVE FOR MY *FAMILY*-- AND BY THAT I DON'T MEAN JUST MY *BLOOD* RELATIVES...

"...BUT MY *BLOOD LINE.*

"MY *WHITE, AMERICAN* BLOOD LINE."

"I BELIEVE IN MY *WHITE* BROTHERS AND SISTERS...

"...THOSE WHO HAVE THE *GUTS* TO SPEAK THE *TRUTH* AND THE *STONES* TO BACK IT UP.

"I BELIEVE I'M *RIGHT*.

"I BELIEVE I'M *HATED* FOR WHAT I BELIEVE.

GWYNETH HONEY...

...ABOUT WHAT YOU SAW THIS MORNING...

...I'M SORRY.

I WISH I COULD KEEP YOU AWAY FROM THAT TYPE OF THING.

BUT THE TRUTH IS, I CAN'T.

NOT AS LONG AS THIS COUNTRY REMAINS IN THE HANDS OF THOSE THAT SEEK TO DESTROY IT.

THOSE THAT OPENLY SPIT THEIR BILE IN THE FACES OF GOOD PEOPLE THAT LIVE BY GOD'S LAWS --LAWS THAT ARE WRITTEN IN THE HOLY BIBLE.

WE LIVE BY THOSE LAWS. I DON'T THINK THEY'RE TOO HARSH.

MAYBE IT'S BECAUSE I'M NOT SO ARROGANT AS TO THINK I KNOW BETTER THAN GOD.

RACE MIXING IS A SIN IN THE EYES OF THE LORD...

AND "THE WEED OF SIN BEARS BITTER FRUIT."

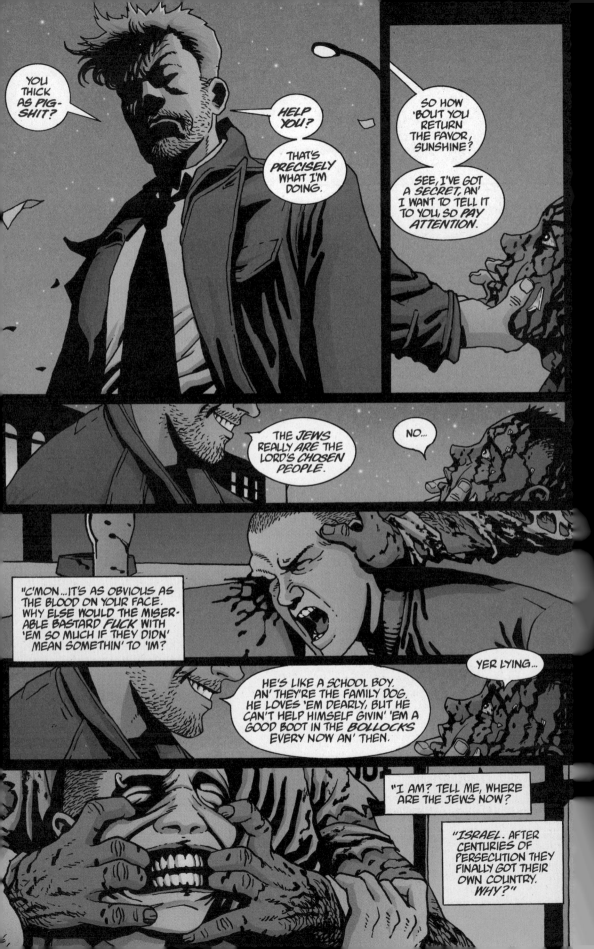

'CAUSE A *FUCKING MANIAC* WITH A TALENT FOR BRINGIN' OUT THE WORST IN PEOPLE AN' 'AVIN' 'EM BELIEVE IT'S THEIR BEST, *KILLED SIX MILLION* OF 'EM.

"THE JEWS WOULDN'T 'AVE THEIR BLEEDIN' *PROMISED LAND,* IF IT WEREN'T FOR *HITLER.*"

FILE THAT UNDER "*MYSTERIOUS WAYS.*"

THAT'S THE *SECRET.*

AN' THE *FAVOR?*

I WANT YOU TO LET THE FUEHRER IN ON IT WHEN YOU MEET 'IM.

"I BELIEVE THE GOVERNMENT FEARS ME.

"I BELIEVE IT SHOULD."

"I BELIEVE THAT PEOPLE *FEAR* THE FEDERAL GOVERNMENT, WHEN IT SHOULD BE THE *OTHER WAY AROUND.*"

YES?

DID YOU HEAR THAT, FREDO? MY FAVORITE WORD, COMING FROM THE MOUTH OF SUCH A *DELICIOUS* LITTLE GIRL.

SO, YOU PRECIOUS LITTLE ROSEBUD...

...IS YOUR *FATHER* HOME?

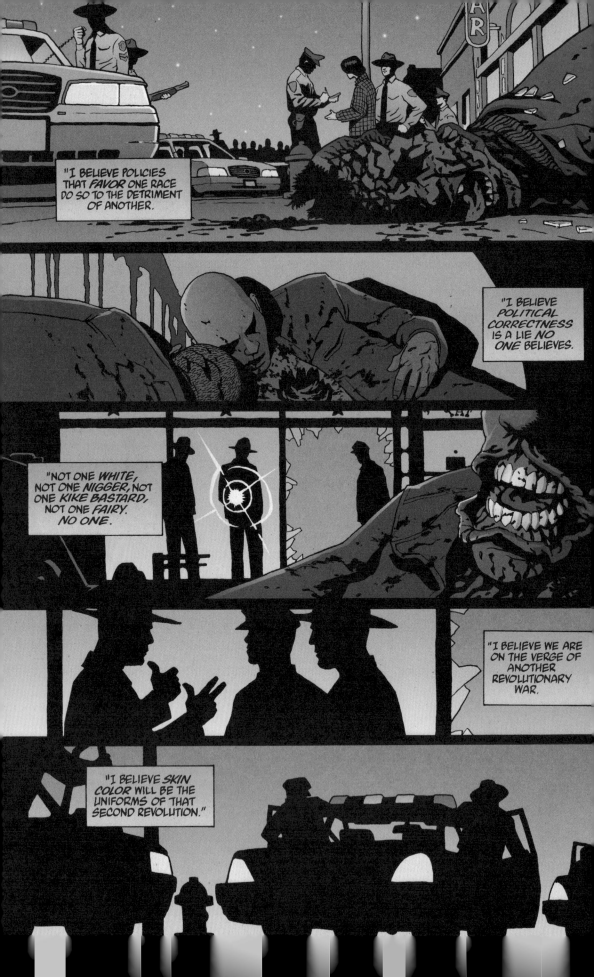

NOW ELLISON...

...WHAT ARE WE GOING TO DO ABOUT MY *PROBLEM?*

CALL ME *S.W.,* ALL MY FRIENDS DO...RIGHT, FREDO?

PROBLEM, MR. MANOR?

THAT'S CORRECT, MR. MANOR.

CORRECT-- GOOD WORD. WE NEED SOME CORRECTION HERE.

WHAT? BUT YOU--

--GAVE YOU THE MONEY TO BUY GUNS. *ISRAELI* GUNS, MANUFACTURED BY MANOR WORLDWIDE INDUSTRIES.

THAT DOESN'T MAKE ANY SENSE.

YOU *ASSUME* TO TELL *ME* HOW TO CONDUCT BUSINESS?

I OWN A SUCCESSFUL HAMBURGER FRANCHISE, DON'T I FREDO?

COUNTING A RECENT ACQUISITION, YOU OWN FOUR, SIR.

"AND I OWN CATTLE RANCHES AND SLAUGHTERHOUSES THAT SUPPLY THE MEAT, RIGHT?"

"YES, SIR."

STOP WITH THE *SIR*. WHO AM I *REALLY*, FREDO?

YOU'RE S.W. MANOR. ONE OF THE RICHEST MEN IN THE WORLD.

RICH IS AN INSIGNIFICANT WORD TO DESCRIBE WHAT I *AM*.

--OR *EYES*-- AND BE DONE WITH THIS.

I'M PREPARED TO DO THAT.

BUT I DON'T THINK IT WOULD FEEL *GOOD.*

AND I *NEED* TO FEEL *GOOD.* I NEED...

...TO CUM IN SOMEONE'S MOUTH.

CORRECTION. NOT *JUST* ANYBODY'S...

YOURS, ELLISON...

OR HERS.

*ZZIP*

89

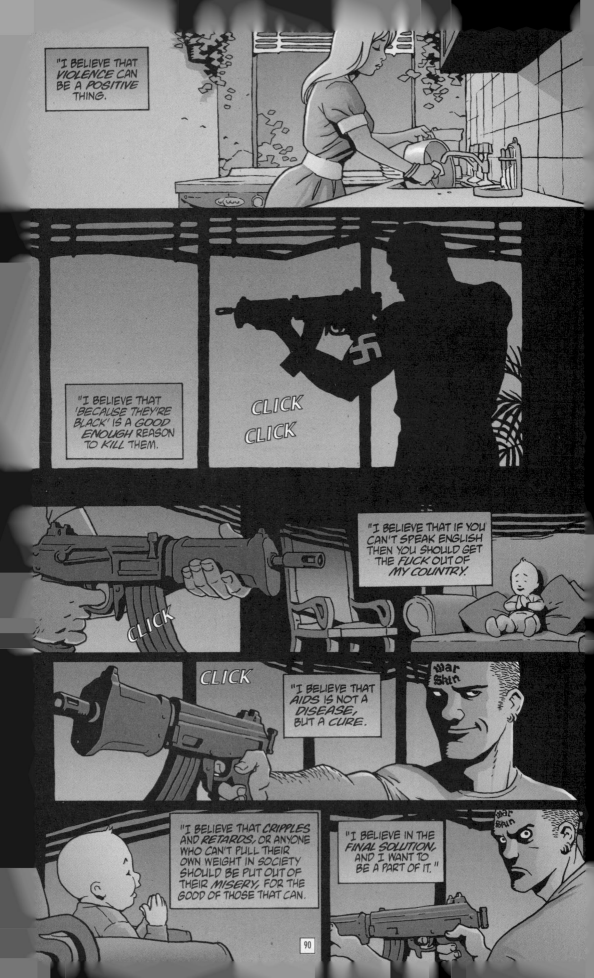

"I BELIEVE THAT *VIOLENCE* CAN BE A *POSITIVE* THING.

"I BELIEVE THAT 'BECAUSE THEY'RE *BLACK*' IS A *GOOD ENOUGH* REASON TO *KILL* THEM.

CLICK
CLICK

CLICK

"I BELIEVE THAT IF YOU CAN'T SPEAK ENGLISH THEN YOU SHOULD GET THE *FUCK* OUT OF *MY COUNTRY.*

CLICK

"I BELIEVE THAT *AIDS* IS NOT A *DISEASE,* BUT A *CURE.*

"I BELIEVE THAT *CRIPPLES* AND *RETARDS,* OR ANYONE WHO CAN'T PULL THEIR OWN WEIGHT IN SOCIETY SHOULD BE PUT OUT OF THEIR *MISERY,* FOR THE GOOD OF THOSE THAT CAN.

"I BELIEVE IN THE *FINAL SOLUTION,* AND I WANT TO BE A PART OF IT."

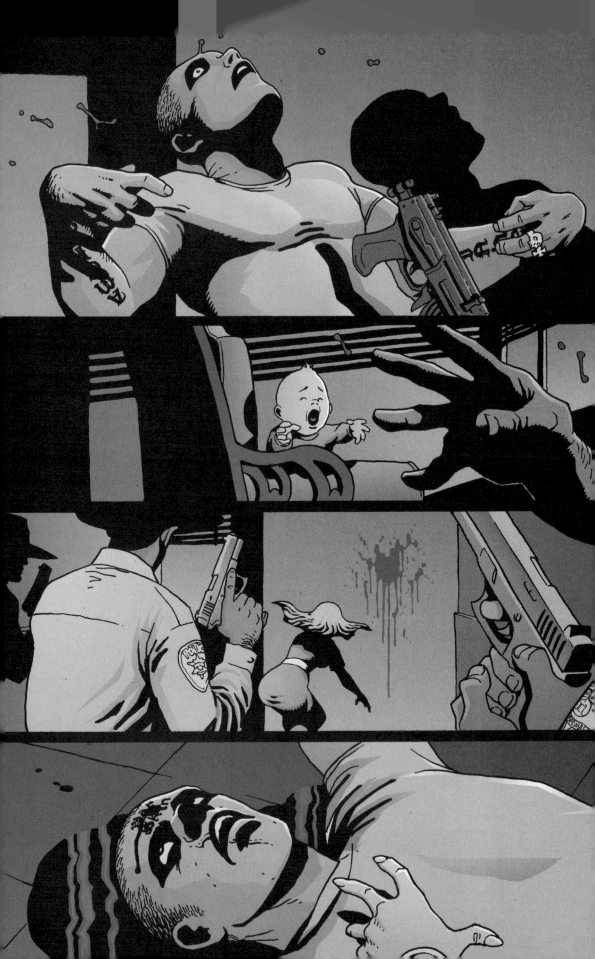

HOMO-SEXUALITY IS A SIN IN THE EYES OF THE LORD.

end

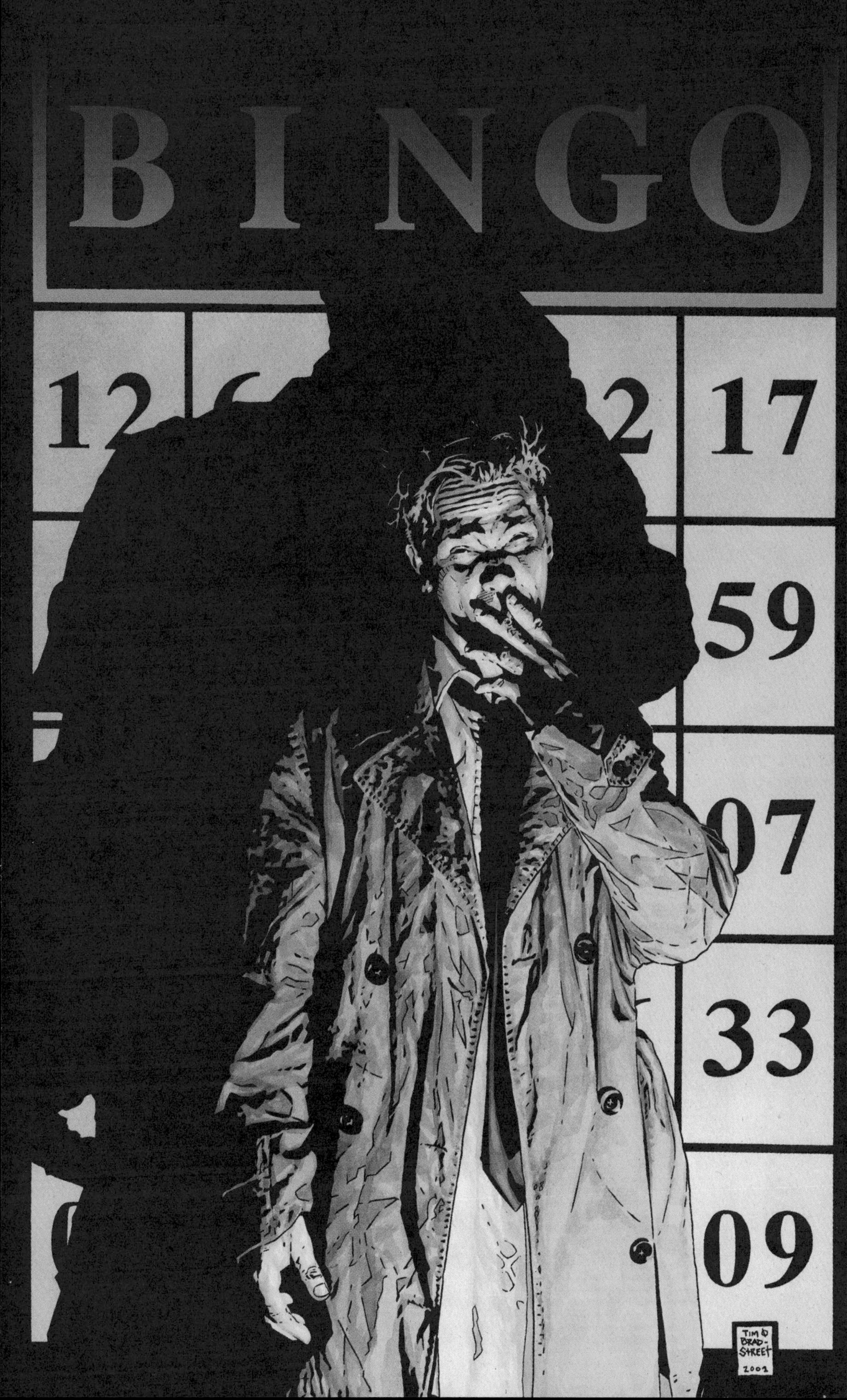
BINGO
12
17
59
07
33
09
TIM BRAD-STREET

...YOU LOOKIN' FOR A DATE?

GAS →

NO...

...BUT I DO 'AVE AN HOUR OR SO TO MURDER.

A *WHOLE* HOUR?

THAT'S GONNA COST YOU.

TIME WELL SPENT, RIGHT?

I PROMISE.

COMING FROM *YOUR* PRECIOUS LITTLE MOUTH...

...THAT'S *VERY* PROMISING.

SO SHALL WE SHOVE OFF, GET SOME MONEY, AN' GET DOWN TO OUR *DIRTY BUSINESS*?

COOL BEANS. THERE'S AN *ATM* JUST UP THE BLOCK.

A WHA?

*ATM--* A BANK MACHINE?

IS THERE? LOVELY. PITY I DON' 'AVE A BANK ACCOUNT.

WHAT? HOW YOU S'POSED TO GET ANY MONEY THEN?

I 'AVE MY WAYS.

GOOD FOR *YOU*, BUT I AIN'T GOIN' THERE.

NOW NOW, ROBBERY AIN'T *ME* GAME. NO STICK-UP KID HERE.

BUT, A TENDERLOIN SUCH AS YOU DON' COME CHEAP, AN' I'M A BIT LIGHT.

SO WHAT SAY WE SEPARATE SOME FOLKS FROM THEIR DOLLARS THE OLD-FASHIONED WAY?

AN' HOW'S THAT?

JESUS CHRIST, SIX WINS IN A ROW!

THAT ENOUGH TO GET IN YA KNICKERS?

DEPENDS WHAT YOU WANT TO *DO* WHEN YOU GET THERE.

RIGHT. BEST PLAY *ANOTHER* CARD...

HELL YEAH. YOU'RE ON A LUCKY STREAK.

CAN'T SAY I'VE BEEN ON MANY BEFORE...

TONIG

WHAT ARE *YOU* LOOKIN' AT?

I DON'T THINK THESE OLD BIRDS APPROVE.

TESUS SAVES

I DON'T CARE *WHAT* THEY THINK, LOVER. DO *YOU?*

LEMME SEE...

THEY THINK...

"B" ELEVEN.

...THAT WE DON'T *BELONG* HERE. THAT WE'RE INVADERS.

THAT'S COOL...

ON THE CONTRARY, THEY THINK WE'RE LIKE *RATS,* OR *ROACHES*-- VERMIN, COME TO *INFEST* THEIR TIDY LITTLE HOME.

"I" TWENTY-ONE.

THEY THINK THAT AFTER LEADING LONG, *MISERABLY UNFULFILLING* LIVES, THEY *DESERVE* BETTER.

THEY THINK THIS IS ALL THE FUN THEY 'AVE, AN' WE'RE *RUINING* IT. THAT THIS BLOODY GAME IS THE ONLY THING THEY LOOK FORWARD TO WEEK IN AND WEEK OUT.

"*N*" THIRTY-FIVE.

TONIGHT BING...

THEY THINK YOU'RE *BEAUTIFUL*, AN' THEY *HATE* YOU FOR IT...

"*G*" FIFTY-THREE.

THEY THINK THEIR CHILDREN ARE *SELFISH*...

...BUT THAT THEY WERE OBVIOUSLY *BETTER PARENTS* THAN *YOURS* WERE.

...THAT I'M ONE *DEGENERATE BASTARD*...

...AN' THEY WISH THAT WAS *THEIR HAND*, 'STEAD A YERS.

THEY THINK YOU AN' ME--WE'RE GONNA DO SOME *RIGHT NASTY* THINGS TO EACH OTHER 'FORE THE NIGHT IS OVER...

...AN' THAT IT'S BEEN TOO *FUCKING* LONG SINCE THEY'VE EXPERIENCED *ANYTHING NASTY.*

THEY WISH THEY WAS *YOUNG* AGAIN, SO'S THEY COULD KISS, LICK, SUCK, AN' BE TOUCHED.

"O" SIXTY-NINE.

SWEAT, DRIP, OOZE, MELT AROUND A BODY THAT SETS YOU DELIRIOUSLY ON FIRE BUT IS *INFINITELY HOTTER* THAN YOURS. THEY *NEVER* GOT ENOUGH OF THAT, BUT *WHO* DOES?

SO LUV, TA ANSWER YOUR QUESTION...

...NO. I BLOODY WELL DON' GIVE A *TOSS* WHAT THEY THINK.

BINGO.

ANDERBIL
HOTEL

'ERE WE ARE.

THIS *YOUR* HOTEL?

NOT *MINE*, BUT YOU LIKE?

IT'LL *WORK*.

THAS' ALL I ASK OF ANYTHING, REALLY.

SO 'OW LONG YOU BEEN IN YOUR PARTICULAR LINE OF WORK?

FEW YEARS. MONEY'S GOOD.

*FUCK,* MONEY'S *GREAT*.

LOOKIN' LIKE *YOU DO,* I IMAGINE IT IS.

Y'KNOW, THAT'S A COMMON MISPERCEPTION.

WHA?

THE *LOOKS* THING. SURE, I KNOW I'M *HOT,* BUT IT'S *PERFORMANCE* THAT COUNTS.

TRUST ME, I'VE SEEN GIRLS --*FUCK*-- *CRACK WHORES* WITH ROTTEN TEETH, STINKIN' LIKE PISS --*SUCK OFF* SOME COKED-UP HOLLYWOOD *DOUCHE BAG* IN THIRTY SECONDS.

S'THAT GOOD?

YOU EVER DO COKE?

RIGHT. THAT *IS* GOOD.

AN' THAT'S ALL THIS IS. BUSINESS.

HERE I THOUGHT YOU FANCIED ME...

I DO. TOO BAD I DIDN'T MEET YOU ON MY NIGHT OFF.

SO MY POINT IS, LOOKS'LL GET YOU IN, BUT IT'S HOW YOU DO THE JOB THAT GETS YOU BUSINESS.

HEH... JOHN. FUNNY THAT.

WHEN'S THAT?

HONEY... I DON' EVER TAKE NIGHTS OFF.

WHAT'S YOUR NAME, ANYWAY?

IF YOU SAY SO... JOHN. WHAT YOU WANNA CALL ME?

KITTY'LL DO.

KNOCK KNOCK

THIS AIN'T YOUR ROOM?

NO.

'ELLO, TURRO.

CONSTANTINE.

WHO'S THIS GUY?

C'MON LUV, YA KNEW WHEN WE WALKED IN A PLACE LIKE THIS, IT'D BE *CRAWLIN'* WITH *BEDBUGS*.

WE *BITE*, TOO.

YOU A *COP*?

F.B.I. YOU A *WHORE*?

SEX THERAPIST.

WHAT *STINKS* IN HERE?

A FRESH LAID, MEAN *SHIT*.

YOU AIN'T THAT *FRESH OR MEAN*, TURRO. WHAT'S WITH THE MUSTACHE, NOW?

UNDERCOVER-- DOGFIGHTS. YOU *LIKE?*

MUSTACHE, *YES.* EVERY- THING UNDER IT, *NO.*

HEY PAL, I'M YOUR *BUDDY.*

IF ONLY THAT WERE TRUE. SEE, MY *BUDDIES...*

...END UP AS *BODIES.*

AND YOUR *ENEMIES?*

*WORSE.*

OOOOHH.

PISS OFF.

FUCK YOU.

WHO'S FIRST?

WHAT?

WHICH ONE OF YOU GUYS AM I DOIN' *FIRST*?

HA! BABY, IF *I* FUCKED YOU, YOU WOULDN'T BE IN ANY SHAPE FOR *SECONDS*.

I *LIKE* THE SOUND OF THAT...

THEN YOU'D ABSOLUTELY *LOVE* HOW IT FEELS.

MMMM... SHOW ME YOUR *COCK*. I BET IT'S *BIG*...

THAT S'POSED TO TURN ME *ON*? JESUS CHRIST, YOU--

--I THOUGHT WE'D DO YA...

...TOGETHER.

'SAT ALL RIGHT, KITTY?

YOU GOT SIX HUNDRED, LET'S GO.

WHAT YA SAY, TURRO? MY TREAT.

WHAT'RE YOU-- GAY?

HMM. *I'M* LOOKIN' AT THIS LOVELY GIRL HERE, AN' I'M GETTIN' A BIT HOT AN' BOTHERED, CAN BARELY WAIT TO HAVE AT HER.

YOU, ON THE OTHER HAND, SEEM COOL TO THE PROSPECT.

SO WAS YOUR QUESTION JUS' *THAT*--OR A PROPOSITION?

THE ASS-HOLE'LL COST YOU ANOTHER HUNDRED.

HOL' ON LUV, YOU JUS' SAID SIX, 'IM INCLUDED.

HAHA...YOU'RE A REGULAR BENNY-*FUCKIN'*-HILL.

YEAH? I EVER TELL YOU 'BOUT THE *WORST* BLOW-JOB I EVER GOT?

IT WAS *GREAT*, RIGHT?

SO YOU'VE MET *HER?*

PICK AN END.

'OW 'BOUT WE FLIP A COIN?

*HEADS* I WIN?

YOU AIN'T GONNA LOSE WITH *TAILS* EITHER, HONEY.

SOMEONE *SPECIFIC* IN MIND?

OF COURSE.

ANYONE I *KNOW?*

KNOW *OF.*

SO SOME OF THE *GUTS* THAT WAS SPILLED IN HIGHWATER BELONGED TO THAT *FERMIN WIDOW?*

NOT *EXACTLY.*

WELL, I COULD NEVER GET HER TO *OPEN UP.* YOU MUST BE QUITE THE *CHARMER.*

YOU *KNEW* ALL ALONG--

--WHO WAS *REALLY BEHIND* YOU ENDIN' UP BEHIND BARS? SURE AS *SHIT* I DID. BUT WHAT I DIDN'T HAVE WAS *PROOF*--AN' EVEN IF I DID...

YOU CAN'T TOUCH HIM.

NO. I CAN'T.

AND I CAN'T DO THIS.

ALL COCK, NO BALLS.

YEAH.

THAT'S WHAT IT IS.

IS IT? I GOT ME A NOSE TOO, SUNSHINE, AND IT'S CATCHIN' THE ODOR...

...OF LOVE.

FIDELITY.

GUILT. THAT ODD PIECE OF GRAY MATTER THAT PUTS THE BRAKES ON WHEN THE RED MATTER IS *SCREAMIN'* BLOODY MURDER AND THREATENS TO LIVE IN A GLORIOUSLY *DESPICABLE* MOMENT.

IS A NASTY LITTLE *SWITCH*, INSTALLED BY THE *CREATOR*. WHAT *SEPARATES* US FROM THE ANIMALS, REALLY.

SO 'OW'D *YOU* GET ONE, FRANK?

KISS MY *ASS*.

HE REALLY IS *GAY*?

NO, MY DEAR KITTY, 'IS LOVE RUNS *TABOO*, A BIT MORE *CRIMINAL* THAN THAT.

CONSTANTINE?

WHA?

YOU'RE DEAD.

THAT A THREAT?

NO.

IT'S A FACT.

OFFICIALLY? YOU WERE KILLED IN THAT RIOT BACK IN PRISON.

THAT'S A REAL ADVANTAGE I HAVE.

THAT'S WHY I'M TELLING YOU.

CHEERS.

I'M NOT FROM *HERE*.

I'M FROM *THERE*. THE OTHER SIDE OF THE POND.

THE APTLY NAMED-- THOUGH BY WHAT GIT I HAVEN'T THE FAINTEST-- "OLD WORLD."

IDIØT FLESH

LIVE AT THE MILE
03 | 02 | 1996 | 22 PM

AN' US GOOD CITIZENS OF THE OLD WORLD, WE CALL THIS PLACE--FUNNY ENOUGH--THE *NEW WORLD.*

*WHY,* YOU ASK?

BECAUSE IT DIDN' 'AVE A HISTORY, 'TIL *WE* ARRIVED AN ESTAB- LISHED ONE.

PRESUMPTUOUS, YES, BUT YOU'LL EXCUSE US THAT, SEEIN' 'OW ANY EFFECTS WE 'AVE ON THE WORLD-- OLD OR NEW--ARE SADLY IN THE *PAST*.

SO IT'S *VICARIOUS LIVING* FOR US GOOD CITIZENS NOW, WITH THE OCCASIONAL *VIAGRA* DOLED OUT TO OUR *IMPOTENT* OFFICIALS FROM THE WHITE HOUSE CHEMIST...

...AN' WHEN YOU AIN'T GETTIN' A *SQUIRT* A *NOTHIN'*?

*SLOPPY SECONDS* CAN BE QUITE THE RARE TREAT.

SEE, OUR BETTER DAYS LAY IN THE *DROOPY ARSE BEHIND* US, NOT THE *DOUGHY PAUNCH* RIGHT IN FRONT.

S'WHY WE NURTURED AN' SPREAD ONE OF OUR GREATEST CONTRIBUTIONS TO HUMANITY...

...SO WE'D *ALWAYS* HAVE A PLACE...

...TO BE YOUNG AN' HARD AGAIN.
Chasing Demons
brian azzarello writer
giuseppe camuncoli penciller
inker pps. 12-14,17,21
cameron stewart inker
lee loughridge colorist clem robins letterer
tim bradstreet cover artist
zachary rau ass't ed. will dennis editor
LIQUEUR
SALE $6.95
OPEN

BLOODY FUCKIN' HELL...

ACHK!

SORRY 'BOUT THAT, BUDDY.

MY SINUSES-- THIS WEATHER'S MURDERIN' 'EM.

WON' BE JUS' THE WEATHER, YOU GAK ON ME AGAIN LIKE THAT.

TAKE IT EASY.

KILKENNY

LOS ANGELA

SEBA

TAKE IT EASY? I SHOULD BE TAKIN' ME MEDICINE AFTER ALL THE NASTY VIRAL BITS YA JUS' BLEW IN MY DIRECTION.

YOU NEED MEDICINE?

YOU A DOCTOR?

MY MOTHER WANTED ME TO BE ONE.

AN' WHAT WAS SHE?

DELUSIONAL. ALWAYS THINKIN' ABOUT TOMORROW. REALITY... WAS SOMETHIN' SHE NEVER QUITE GOT HER MIND AROUND.

WHISKEY?

EH?

YER *MEDICINE*-- WHISKEY?

THE DOCTOR'S *ORDERIN'*.

YEAH ...A DROP A WHISKEY'LL DO.

HEY MIKE-- COUPLE BUSHMILLS?

CHEERS.

GOOD TO SEE YOU *AGAIN*.

?

DON' FUCKIN' SAY YOU DON' *KNOW* ME.

STANLEY, IF YOU'RE *IMPLYING*--

--I'M NOT IMPLYING *ANYTHING*, SEAN.

IT'S CALLED *GOSSIP.* MEAN-SPIRITED-- COMES WITH AN *AGENDA.*

JUST LITTLE PEOPLE OUT TO GAIN AN INCH OR TWO BY CUTTING DOWN THOSE WHO SEEM TALLER.

PARTY TALK AND PETTY VICES.

THE THINGS *I* HEAR CAN'T EVEN *REMOTELY* COMPARE TO THE THINGS...

...*YOU* DO.

CONFESSIONS. HORRIBLE, EMBARRASSING THINGS PEOPLE WOULDN'T DARE TELL ANOTHER SOUL...

THE *TRUTH* ABOUT THEMSELVES.

LET'S NOT WASTE ANY MORE TIME, FATHER.

WORD FOR DELICIOUS WORD...

...TELL ME THEIR *SINS.*

133

WHA' A SURPRISE...

?

I MEAN, YOU DON' *LOOK* LIKE THE *MARRYIN'* TYPE.

THAT AIN'T *BLOOD,* WALLY, YOU *ASSHOLE...*

...IT'S DRIED KETCHUP.

THE *HELL* IT IS. IT'S HER *BLOOD.*

ON MY HANDS.

HAVE A PINT!

SO GO *WASH* 'EM.

I DUNNO... LOOKS LIKE BLOOD TA *ME...*

TWENTY-FIVE YEARS...

BACK IN *SEVENTY-SIX?* WALLY *SHOT* HIS MISSUS IN THE *BELLY.* THEY WERE BOTH PRETTY *GASSED.* BEEN AT IT ALL DAY, WHEN HE DECIDED TO CLEAN HIS GUN.

WALLY DIDN'T KNOW IT WAS *LOADED,* TOO.

THAS' AN ALIBI I'LL 'AVE TO *REMEMBER.*

HE SURE CAN'T FORGET.

TWENTY-FIVE YEARS...

SEEMS LIKE YESTERDAY.

YESTERDAY?

YESTERDAY.

ALL ME TROUBLES SEEMED SO FAR AWAY...

--SAY THAT AGAIN.

WHAT YOU JUST SAID --WHAT *SHE* SAID.

"I FIND HIM *LOATHSOME*, FATHER. *ALL THE TIME*, AND ON *EVERY LEVEL*. THAT WON'T CHANGE. I *SWEAR* TO YOU."

LOATHSOME... NOW *THAT'S* A WORD.

IS IT A *SIN*?

I THINK WHAT SHE'S GOING THROUGH IS MORE *COMPLEX* THAN THAT.

SURE, SURE. OF COURSE. SO I GUESS MY QUESTION *REALLY* IS, DID YOU *ABSOLVE* HER?

I GAVE HER *ADVICE*--

--DID YOU SAY--

"THE LORD FORGIVES YOU FOR *ALL YOUR SINS*"?

YES.

--HELP ME-EE-EE ♫

YEEAAHH ♪

CHRIST, I FUCKIN' *HATE* THAT BAND...

WELL THAT DON' KEEP THEIR TUNES FROM SWIMMIN' AROUN' UP IN YER SKULL.

FUCKIN' AYE. WHAT SAY WE DROWN THE MISERABLE LOT OF 'EM?

MIKE!

WHY IS IT, YA THINK, I CAN'T REMEMBER WHAT I HAD FOR ME SUPPER...

...YET I KNOW ALL THE WORDS TO A DOPEY SONG I AIN'T HEARD IN AGES?

BEATS THE PISS OUTTA *ME*. BUT THE BRAIN'S ONLY SO *BIG*, Y'KNOW?

MAYBE YER *MEMORY?* IT SIFTS THROUGH ALL THE *GARBAGE* --GOOD AND *BAD,* AND HANGS ONTO THE SHIT THAT COULD HELP YOU OUT DOWN THE ROAD.

SO THAT YER *PAST?* REALLY ONLY MEANS SOMETHING IN RELATION TO YER *FUTURE.*

MEMORY'S A *CRAZY DEVIL* --BUT IT KEEPS US *SANE.*

SPEAKING OF WHICH, FREDO HAS A *CHECK* FOR YOU.

SEE YOU NEXT WEEK.

YOU *BROKE* THE *SACRED TRUST* YOU SHARE WITH YOUR *PARISHIONERS* AND YOUR *GOD* FOR *MONEY.*

*SIMPLE* AS *THAT.*

AN' FATHER?

MY REASON FOR SEEING YOU HAS *CHANGED.*

THAT *"I'M SORRY"* IS A LIE WE TELL SO WE CAN FORGET OUR *PAST.*

NOW? I ENJOY THE *REAFFIRMATION* OF THE *UGLY TRUTH* YOUR POOR CATALOG OF A BRAIN WON'T LET YOU *ESCAPE.*

I REMEMBER YOU NOW, SQUIRE.

YEAH? WELL I AIN'T SEEN *YOU* BEFORE IN MY *LIFE*.

C'MON...IN *DUBLIN* A FEW YEARS BACK, YOU WAS HEAVIER--FAT, ACTUALLY--

--AN' IN *BRIGHTON*, ON A STORMY SUMMER NIGHT LACED WITH *BENNIES*.

IN *SAN FRANCISCO* ON A SUNDAY AFTERNOON, YOU *ATTEMPTED*-- UNSUCCESSFULLY-- TO EXPLAIN THE RULES OF AMERICAN FOOTBALL.

AN' *NEW YORK.* JESUS, THE TIMES WE'VE 'AD THERE.

YEAH, WE'VE MET BEFORE. *COUNTLESS* TIMES.

IN *COUNTLESS PLACES,* JUST LIKE *THIS*.

WE NEVER LOOK THE SAME *OUTSIDE*.

BUT *INSIDE*?

CHEERS.

END

# Ashes & Dust in the City of Angels
### part one

**Brian Azzarello**, writer    **Marcelo Frusin**, artist

Lee Loughridge
colors

Clem Robins
letters

Tim Bradstreet
cover

Zachary Rau
assistant editor

Will Dennis
editor

GODDAMN... THAT SMELL.

YOU CAN SAY THAT AGAIN.

LIKE BACON.

MAKES ME HUNGRY.

WELL, THE VEGETABLES'LL BE READY ANY SECOND, IF YOU CAN WAIT.

VEGETABLES --WITNESSES, YOU MEAN?

NO. WAS JUST A JOKE.

OH.

HA HA.

WHAT ABOUT WITNESSES?

FOR WHAT IT'S WORTH, I GOT A HANDFUL.

WHEN IN ROME, HUH?

I WANT TO TALK TO THEM.

ALL RIGHT. I'LL HAVE MY OFFICE CONTACT YOU WHEN WE DO THE INTERVIEWS. SHOULD BE WITHIN FORTY-EIGHT HOURS.

SOUNDS *SWELL.* ONLY I'M GETTING STARTED *TONIGHT.*

THAT'S *NOT* GOING TO HAPPEN.

NO?

NO. WELCOME TO *L.A. POLICE PROCEDURE 101,* AGENT TURRO. SOME OF THE WITNESSES--

DO ME A *BIG* FAVOR. CALL 'EM *SUSPECTS*--

--ARE RICH, FAMOUS, OR BOTH.

THE *MINUTE* I TELL THEM WE'RE GOING DOWNTOWN FOR QUESTIONING IS THE *SECOND* THEY PULL THEIR CELL PHONES OUT OF THEIR CODPIECES, OR *ASS CHEEKS*--

OR FROM BETWEEN A RACK OF MANMADE *FUNBAGS*--

SURE, AND WHEN WE GET TO THE STATION WE'LL FIND IT *CRAWLING* WITH ATTORNEYS, EACH ONE SINGING THE SAME SONG.

THEN GO CONVINCE THE *SUSPECTS* IT'S THEIR *CIVIC DUTY* TO COOPERATE, AND LEAVE THEIR LAWYERS OUT OF THIS.

150

HI, MILTON.

HI.

MY NAME'S *AGENT* TURRO.

THAT'S A *FUNNY* NAME.

IT IS?

HOW SO?

I MEAN *AGENT.* IT'S NOT LIKE BOB, OR TIM--

--OR MILTON?

I GUESS.

YOU *GUESS.*

WHAT DO YOU *KNOW?*

NOT MUCH.

I'M NOT TALKING ABOUT *IN GENERAL,* MILTON.

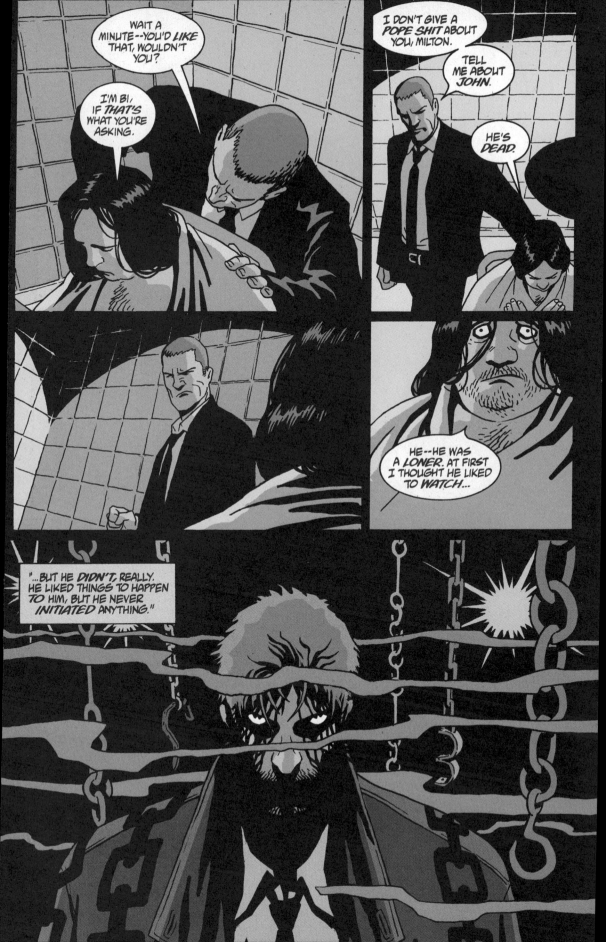

"...AND I REMEMBER, I FELT *SAFE*, BECAUSE I WAS *WET*. AND I WATCHED.

"HE DIDN'T DO *ANYTHING* TO PUT THE FIRE OUT.

HE JUST *STOOD* THERE, AND *BURNED*.

JUST STOOD THERE? *NOBODY* 'ROUND HIM, HOLDIN' A MATCH?

SO MILTON, TELL ME-- YOU SEE A GUY ON FIRE--YOU GET UP, *DO* SOMETHING?

LIFT A FUCKING *FINGER*? RUN AWAY?

157

WHAT? *OUR* CORONER--

--YEAH, YEAH, I'M SURE FLOYD DOES A *GREAT JOB* IN BETWEEN HAIRCUTS, BUT WE'LL HANDLE THIS ONE.

ALONE, OKAY.

I HEAR I GOT A *FRENCH FRY.*

HE'S *ENGLISH*-- IF IT'S *HIM.* I'M *NOT* CONVINCED.

WHY?

'CAUSE I'M *NOT.* LOOK, THIS GUY WAS--IS--A GRADE A-NUMBER-FUCKIN'-ONE *CON MAN.* HE'S TOO OILY TO END UP A LUMP OF COAL.

*YOU* THROW HIM INTO THE FIRE, TURRO?

I'LL CALL YOU WHEN I HAVE SOMETHING.

DON'T *EAT* ANY EVIDENCE.

CAN I ASK YOU AGAIN, WHAT'S IT ABOUT THIS *HORRORSHOW,* GOT YOU FEDS ALL INTERESTED?

NO.

MR. MANOR?

YES, FREDO?

YOUR BATH IS READY.

THANK YOU. I'LL BE UP IN A FEW.

"HE WAS *INSATIABLE.* GOD.

"NEVER...

"...EVER...

"SATISFIED.

"HE MOVED LIKE A TIGER FROM ONE BODY TO THE NEXT, JUST *DEVOURING.*

"*THEIR* PLEASURE? I DOUBT IF HE NOTICED-- OR *CARED*--IF HE *GAVE* THEM ANY.

"BUT *HIS?*

"WAS *ALL* THAT MATTERED."

"IT WAS BEAUTIFUL TO BEHOLD.

# Ashes & Dust in the City of Angels
## PART TWO

**Brian Azzarello**, WRITER       **Marcelo Frusin**, ARTIST

Lee Loughridge
COLORS

Clem Robins
LETTERS

Tim Bradstreet
COVER

Zachary Rau
ASSISTANT EDITOR

Will Dennis
EDITOR

HELL, PEGGY, THAT'S *SOME* STORY.

HE WAS *SOME* MAN, AGENT TURRO.

I'M NOT SO SURE...

NEITHER AM I. THAT'S WHY I SAID *MIGHT*.

SOUNDS LIKE IT.

*FELT* LIKE IT, TOO. HE MIGHT HAVE BEEN EVEN ENOUGH FOR *ME*.

OKAY... MIGHT YOU WANT TO SAY HOW JOHN CONSTANTINE DIED?

HE *BURNED*.

NO SHIT.

NO, I MEAN JOHNNY HAD A *FIRE*...

...YOU EVER HAVE *CANDLE WAX* DRIPPED ON YOUR NAKED BODY, AGENT?

I'M A BIT MORE TRADITIONAL SEXUALLY, PEGGY.

REALLY?

THAT'S NOT WHAT YOUR *EYES* SAY...

"...IT'S *EXHILARATING.* THE HOT WAX..."

"...*HARDENING* AGAINST YOUR *WARM, WET FLESH.*

"SUCH A *RUSH.*"

AAAHHHWWW...

...MORE, SUGAR.

PATIENCE...

...IS A VIRTUE I DON' AVE TIME FOR, IN ME POCKET...

YOU SAYING HE PULLED A *SIMILAR* STUNT, MAYBE? *THAT'S* WHAT CAUSED THE FIRE?

NO.

YOU *CAN'T* UNDERSTAND, CAN YOU?

I'M SAYING JOHNNY'S FIRE WAS *INSIDE*...

...HE WAS CONSUMED BY *DESIRES* SOMEONE LIKE YOU WOULD BE EMBARRASSED EVEN *FANTASIZING* ABOUT...

...HE *BURNED,* AGENT TURRO...

YOU *RANG*, GHOULARDEE?

YEAH FRANK, I RANG. MAKIN' ANY HEADWAY?

OH, YOU BET, PAL. VERY COOPERATIVE GROUP. ALL THE *GUT* SPILLING GOING ON, IT'S LIKE *YOU* WERE THERE.

NOBODY SAW *ANYTHING*, HUH?

THAT DOESN'T SURPRISE ME.

*UNFLAPPABLE* AS ALWAYS.

SO WHAT HAVE *YOU* GOT?

THE WORST DAMN CASE OF *HEARTBURN* I'VE EVER SEEN.

FUNNY.

NO.

I'M *SERIOUS.* DON'T ASK ME HOW...

179

FREDO? IS--

--NOTHING TO WORRY ABOUT, FATHER SEAN.

JUST A LITTLE SCARE.

MR. MANOR IS WAITING FOR YOU IN THE *GAME ROOM*. REMEMBER WHERE THAT IS?

OF COURSE.

YOU SEEMED VERY *CONCERNED* ON THE PHONE.

REALLY?

HOW DO I SEEM *NOW*?

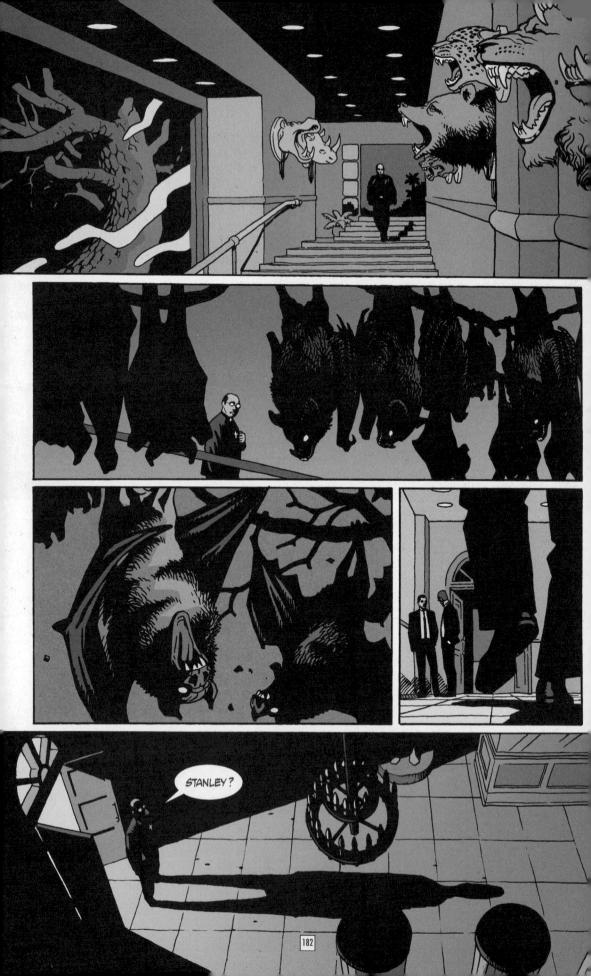

WHAT WAS ATTRACTIVE ABOUT HIM BEFORE STILL WAS--AND THAT'S *DANGEROUS*, MAKES YOU IGNORE THE *OBVIOUS*.

YOU EVER DATE AN EX?

NO. MY EXES LIKE TO STAY THAT WAY.

WHY DO I BELIEVE *THAT?* ANYWAY, WHAT WE THOUGHT WAS A *FRESH START?*--

--TURNED OUT TO BE THE SAME *ROTTEN* RELATIONSHIP?

EXACTLY.

EH, YOU *NEVER KNOW.*

SO YOU TAKE YOUR LUMPS, AN' CHALK IT UP. IT WON'T HAPPEN AGAIN, RIGHT?

"THE SPIRIT IS WEAK..."

"...WHEN THE FLESH IS WILLING."

STANLEY...

BEHIND YOU, FATHER SEAN.

AND IF YOU PERSIST IN CALLING ME STANLEY...

...I'LL CAVE IN YOUR SKULL.

CRYSTAL?

YES, S.W.

GOOD BOY. NOW...

...FIX YOURSELF A DRINK, AND FRESHEN MINE UP WHILE YOU'RE AT IT.

NOT THAT I EXPECT A MAN WITH YOUR FAITH-IMPOSED *LIMITATIONS* TO FULLY COMPREHEND WHAT I'M GOING THROUGH...

SCRATCH THAT...YOU *MIGHT.* THOSE *LIMITATIONS,* VIEWED IN A MIRROR, COULD BE CONSIDERED A FORM OF *SELF-TORTURE,* NO?

YOU'VE *LOST* ME, S.W.

*LOST*-- PRECISELY THE WORD I NEEDED TO HEAR. SEE, I'VE *LOST* SOMETHING I DIDN'T KNOW I HAD...

...AND I FEEL SO VERY *LOST* WITHOUT IT.

THAT'S *IRONY* FOR YOU, HMM?

THIS INTRUDER, WAS HE A *THIEF?*

YES HE WAS.

THE *WORST* POSSIBLE KIND.

188

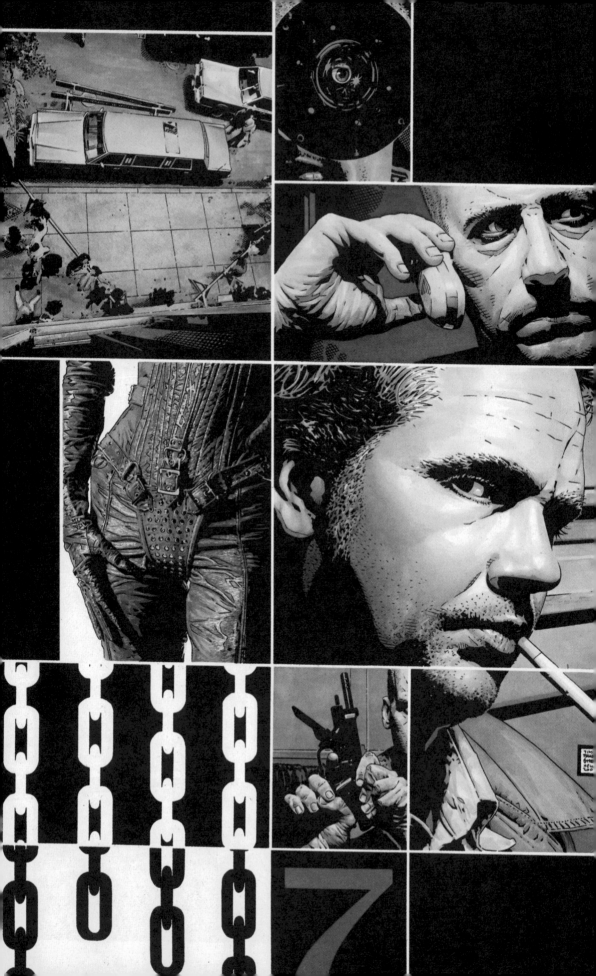

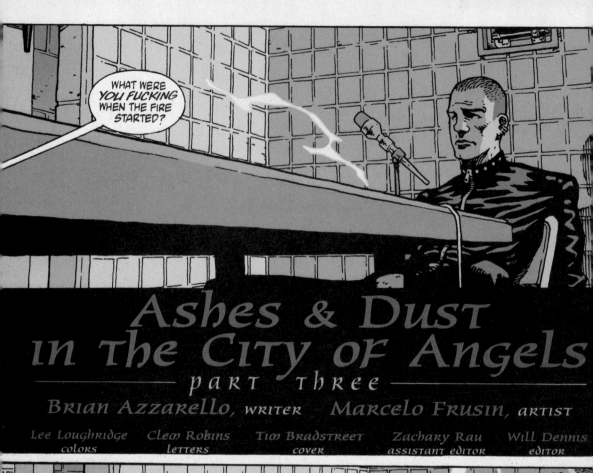

WHAT WERE *YOU FUCKING* WHEN THE FIRE STARTED?

# Ashes & Dust in the City of Angels
## part three

**Brian Azzarello**, WRITER   **Marcelo Frusin**, ARTIST

Lee Loughridge
colors

Clem Robins
letters

Tim Bradstreet
cover

Zachary Rau
assistant editor

Will Dennis
editor

I WASN'T. THIS STUCK-UP HOLLYWOOD *BITCH,* I THOUGHT SHE NEEDED SOME *DISCIPLINE.*

EVER SINCE SHE WON THAT GOLDEN GLOBE, BEEN ACTIN' LIKE HER *SHIT DON' STINK.*

WELL LEMME TELL YA, WHEN I WAS PULLIN' THEM *BENWA BALLS* OUT HER *ASS?* THEY SURE--

--THE WAITER?

YEAH, I WAS THE WAITER.

IN STONE CITY? THE CHUCK SEAGAL PICTURE, ONE ABOUT THE LAWYER WHO'S FRAMED BY HIS CLIENT? GOES ALL KARATE ON HIS ASS AT THE END?

YEAH MAN, I WAS THE WAITER.

WELL FUCK ME, BUT I DON' REMEMBER NO WAITER.

AN' I DON' CARE ABOUT NO ACTRESS, NO BALLS GOIN' IN THE OUT DOOR, NO QUEER JEW HOLLYWOOD CONSPIRACY, OR A NO-TALENT TURD PLAYIN' A WAITER IN SOME B-MOVIE WHEN HE'S MUCH BETTER SUITED TO BEIN' ONE IN REAL LIFE.

WHAT I DO CARE ABOUT IS A BODY BURNED SO FUCKIN' HOT THAT I GOT A SNOWBALL'S CHANCE IN HELL GETTIN' A DNA READING OFF IT.

THAT'S WHAT I CARE ABOUT.

NOW IF WE'RE DONE TALKING ABOUT YOU--

--AND YOU BETTER BELIEVE WE ARE--

"--LET'S TALK ABOUT *THAT.*"

YOUR *FAITH*, FATHER...DOES IT ALLOW FOR *GHOSTS?*

GHOSTS, P.W.? YOU MEAN SOULS, SPENDING THEIR AFTERLIFE HAUNTING THE LIVING?

HAUNTING ...GOOD WORD.

NO. WHEN SOMEONE DIES, THEIR SOUL IS *JUDGED.* GOOD DEEDS AGAINST THE BAD.

AND DEPENDING WHICH SIDE OF THE LEDGER IS FULLER, YOU EITHER STEP THROUGH THE *PEARLY GATES* OR INTO THE GAPING MAW OF *HELL* FOR *ETERNITY.*

THE SPOON-FED *PARTY LINE.*

NO *EXCEPTIONS?*

THERE IS *PURGATORY.*

MANMADE HOPE FOR THE DIVINELY *HOPELESS.*

YOUR *FAITH*--IT'S ONE OF *THOUSANDS.* HOW DO YOU KNOW YOU'RE BACK-ING THE RIGHT HORSE?

YOU SAID IT YOURSELF: MY *FAITH.*

WHICH SAYS ONCE A SOUL IS *JUDGED*, IT EITHER *WON'T*--

--OR *CAN'T*-- --*COMMUNE* WITH THE *LIVING*.

"WELL FATHER, I *KNOW* YOUR FAITH IS *WRONG*."

YOU MEAN YOU HAVE *FAITH* MY FAITH IS WRONG.

I CHOOSE MY WORDS *VERY* PRECISELY, MEANING I *MEAN* WHAT I SAY.

I *KNOW* YOUR *FAITH* IS *WRONG*.

DIDN'T KNOW MUCH ABOUT THE GUY, REALLY. I TRIED TO STEER CLEAR A 'IM.

WHY'S THAT, GRAHAM?

HE RUBBED ME THE *WRONG WAY*.

LITTLE *CHAFING*?

WHA? NO, *THAT'S* NOT WHAT I MEANT.

"HE WAS A FUCKIN' *NOBODY*, JUST SHOWED UP ON THE SCENE ONE NIGHT, ACTED LIKE HE'D BEEN *DOWN WITH IT* HIS WHOLE LIFE.

"TALKIN' ALL *HIGH* AN' *MIGHTY* ABOUT CLUBS FROM BANGKOK TO BUDAPEST. *BULLSHIT*.

"CONSTANTINE WAS A *PHONY*, BUT THE *BASTARD* WAS ALWAYS THE CENTER OF ATTENTION. *EVERYBODY* RAVED ON AN' ON ABOUT HIS *TECHNIQUE*.

"*FEH*."

FOR A MAN YOU STEERED CLEAR OF, YOU GOT A PRETTY STRONG OPINION OF HIM.

YEAH?

WELL, I GOT A *RIGHT* TO.

JUST *AFTER* HE STARTED HANGING AROUND? I WAS WORKIN' OVER A *REGULAR.*

"LET ME REPHRASE THAT: AN *IRREGULAR.* MOST OF THE MEMBERS, THEY SAY THEY'RE *INTO PAIN.* WELL, THEY'RE *NOT.* THEY GET OFF ON THE *THREAT* OF IT.

"BUT *THIS* PARTICULAR GUY?"

MR. MANOR?

YES FREDO?

BOTH THE HOUSE AND THE GROUNDS ARE SECURE.

YOU FOUND *NOTHING.*

YOU SAID WE *WOULDN'T.*

AND *YOU* SAID YOU WANTED TO BE *SURE.*

SO *ARE* YOU?

YES.

ARE YOU *CERTAIN* YOU *SAW* HIM?

AS CERTAIN AS *YOU* ARE THAT I *DIDN'T.*

WONDERFUL.

THERE'S A *FEEDING* SCHEDULED TONIGHT, WOULD YOU LIKE ME TO--

--POSTPONE IT? *ABSOLUTELY NOT.*

COME NOW, FATHER, LET'S GO FOR A NICE WALK AND *CONTINUE* OUR CONVERSATION.

FREDO, YOU AND THE LADS STAY CLOSE, HMM?

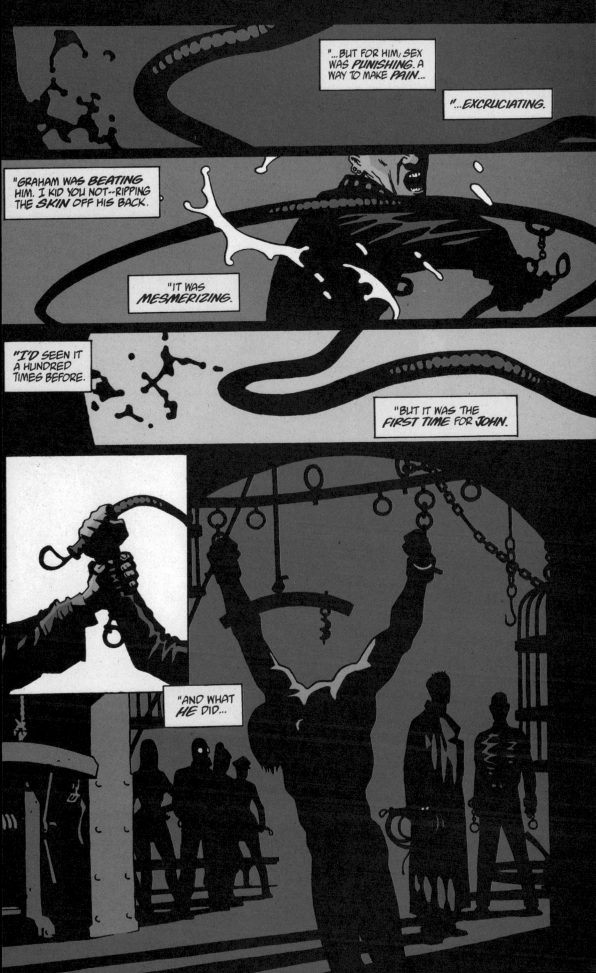

'ELLO *STANLEY*.

HAPPY TO SEE ME, ARE YOU?

CONSTANTINE ...BUT YOU'RE--

--*ALIVE*, MATE. DESPITE YOUR *BEST EFFORTS*.

ALIVE, KICKING...

...AN' ON TO THE *NASTY LITTLE TRICK* YOU TRIED TO PUT OVER ON ME.

IT WAS A GOOD *LAUGH*, WA'NIT, BUT TRUTH IS, I *SURVIVED*.

BUT YOU *DIED* IN PRISON...THE *RIOT*...

ME *DEATH*, WAS A NASTY LITTLE TRICK PUT OVER ON *YOU*.

"HIS VOICE WAS LIKE BUTTER, *SIZZLING* IN A FRYING PAN..."

"LIKE ALL THIEVES, THEY KNEW NOT TO TRUST ANYONE, BUT THEY TRUSTED EACH OTHER, FOR NOTHING'S LIKE *BLOOD ON BLOOD.*

"THEY ALSO TRUSTED A *LIAR.* THIS WAS A MISTAKE, BECAUSE A LIAR IS *NEVER* TO BE TRUSTED.

"NOW THE *SMART* ONE, HE KNEW THAT ONE DAY HE WOULD HAVE TO BE AN HONEST MAN. ON *THAT* DAY HE BECAME HONEST, BUT NO ONE TRUSTED HIM.

"THE *SPECIAL* ONE, HE DIDN'T KNOW ANY BETTER, SO HE FOLLOWED HIS SMART BROTHER. BUT HIS WAS THE *CRUEL HONESTY* OF NATURE, SO *EVERYONE* WAS *AFRAID* OF HIM.

"BUT THE *LUCKY* ONE? HE HAD A HUNCH THAT BEING SMART OR SPECIAL WAS GOOD, BUT BEING *LUCKY* WAS *MUCH BETTER.* AND SINCE THERE IS NO ROOM FOR HONESTY IN LUCK, ANYONE WAS WORTH A CHANCE.

"SO HE REMAINED A THIEF, THOUGH NOT A SPLENDID ONE LIKE BEFORE. HE BECAME *PETTY.*"

A *USELESS, PETTY THIEF,* PEDDLING JUNK OUT OF THE TRUNK OF HIS CAR, UNABLE TO DREAM UP THE NEXT BIG SCORE BECAUSE HE WASN'T SPECIAL...

...NOR WAS HE SMART ENOUGH TO REALIZE HE HAD *NOTHING* TO OFFER ANYONE...

...*EXCEPT* A MAN WHO YOU MIGHT SAY HAD *EVERYTHING.*

A *TORTURED KING.*

THIS *KING* HAD DEALT WITH THE BROTHERS IN THE PAST. BUT THEN WHAT ARE KINGS...

...IF NOT THE *PATRONS* OF *THIEVES?*

NOW THE KING, HE KNEW THAT LUCKY STILL HAD SOMETHING *VALUABLE* HE COULD SELL.

"SO HE MADE LUCKY AN OFFER.

"A *MOUNTAIN* OF *GOLD.*

"AT FIRST, LUCKY *REFUSED.*

"TOO BAD LUCKY HAD A *WIFE,* BECAUSE *SHE* CONVINCED HIM TO DO WHAT THE KING WANTED.

"*SHE* REALIZED THAT IF *HE* ACCEPTED..."

...SHE WOULD BE THE *LUCKY* ONE.

WHAT DID THE KING WANT?

THE *LIAR.*

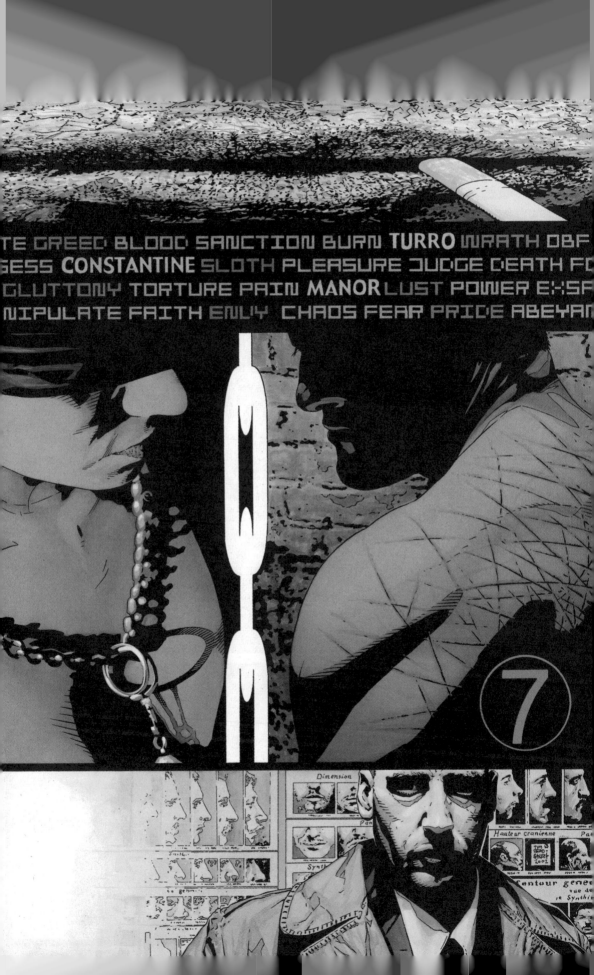

"HE WAS AN *ASSHOLE.* JUST A *NASTY* DUDE.

"LIKE A *CONTROL FREAK.* THINGS *HADDA* BE HIS WAY, AN' IF THEY *WEREN'T?*

HE'D FLY OFF, AN' THE *ONLY* THING THAT COULD CALM HIM DOWN?"

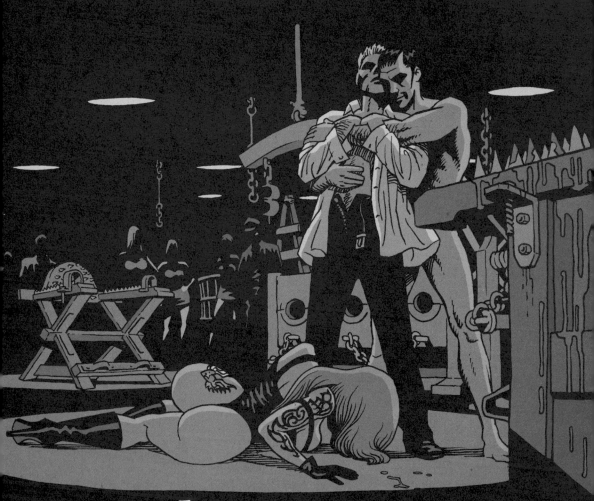

"WAS HIS
BOYFRIEND."

# Ashes & Dust
# in the City of Angels
### part four
**Brian Azzarello,** WRITER     **Marcelo Frusin,** ARTIST

GIVE ME A *NAME.*

NO CAN DO.

NO *FUCKIN' WAY.*

THIS *BOYFRIEND,* HE MIGHT BE A *MURDERER.*

YEAH, AN' IF I TELL YOU HIS NAME...

...HE *WILL BE.*

GIVE ME A *NAME.* WE'LL PROTECT YOU.

NOT FROM *HIM* YOU CAN'T.

*WHO?*

THESE HANDCUFFS ARE TIGHT.

I DON'T HAVE A *KEY.*

I DON'T HAVE A *NAME.*

AAAH! FUCKIN' BITCH!

WHO?

FUCK YOU, TOO!

HE'S CHINESE?

C'MON, LITTLE MAN, WHO?

AAAH!

I'M SITTING OVER HERE. I'M NOT DOING SHIT TO YOU.

AN' I KNOW WHAT HIS NAME IS, STUPID.

YOU CAN'T DO THIS TO ME! I KNOW I GOT RIGHTS!

I NEED YOU TO SAY IT.

FUCKING, STANLEY...

...YOU SHOULDN'T 'AVE.

"FOR OVER TWENTY YEARS..."

...I HATED THIS MAN.

HE PLAYED ME FOR A FOOL WHEN WE WERE BOTH YOUNG...

...AND FOOLISH.

TWENTY YEARS IS A LONG TIME TO HOLD A GRUDGE, S.W.

NO, FATHER--IT ISN'T. SEE, A GRUDGE IS LIKE A TREE--THE ONE THING THAT BECOMES MORE VIBRANT AND ALIVE THAN THE TRANSGRESSION THAT SPAWNED IT. WERE YOU EVER PICKED ON AS A CHILD?

WE ALL WERE.

YOU THINK SO? EVEN THAT BULLY WHO EMBARRASSED YOU IN FRONT OF ALL YOUR OLD CHUMS?

DON'T YOU HAVE A PLACE IN YOUR HEART WHERE THIS TIME, *YOU* END UP ON *TOP?*

IN *MY* HEAD, THAT PLACE HAD JOHN CONSTANTINE *SUFFERING.*

WILLINGLY. PUNISHING HIMSELF.

FOR A TIME, THE PLACE IN MY HEAD BECAME *REALITY.*

SEE MY TREE BORE FRUIT.

BUT THEN I LEARNED HE DIED, AND WITH HIM, MY GRUDGE.

THAT LEFT ME *EMPTY.*

WHEN HE REVEALED HIMSELF TO BE AMONG THE LIVING, I ...

...I COULDN'T *HATE* HIM ANYMORE.

SEE, FATHER...

"... I WANT YOU TO KNOW..."

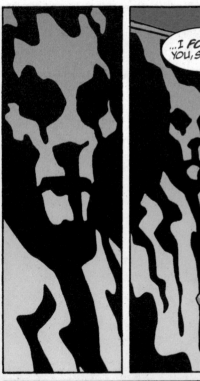

...I *FORGIVE* YOU, STANLEY.

FOR MAKING ME DOUBT MYSELF... TRAIPSING ACROSS THIS *ARSEHOLE* OF A COUNTRY, TRYIN' TO MAKE AMENDS FOR A DEATH YOU BOUGHT. `WAS A CLEVER PLAN.

I'M *IMPRESSED.* THAT'S NOT EASY TO DO.

TO BE HONEST, I MEANT TO KEEP YOU IN PRISON.

RIGHT ENOUGH. BUT THE THING ABOUT YOUR PLAN--THE *BRILLIANCE*...

...KEPT ME *IN,* EVEN WHEN I WAS *OUT.*

HOW YOU FEEL--WHAT'S HAPPENED BETWEEN US-- THESE PAST FEW WEEKS?

I...

I FEEL A BIT *SILLY*...

...I MEAN, YOU GIVE ME THIS LOVELY NEW COAT...

...AN' I 'AVEN'T *ANYTHING* FOR YOU.

THERE'S *NOTHING* I NEED, JOHN.

I HAVE IT *ALL.*

YEAH, YOU DO. EXCEPT...

...HAND ME ME OL' COAT.

CHEERS. I KNEW THIS BIRD ONCE, HAD A STRANGE HABIT--WHEN SHE'D GO ON HOLIDAY?--

--OF BRINGING BACK A BIT OF *SOIL* FROM WHERE SHE'D BEEN.

SHE'D DISPLAY THESE LITTLE SAMPLES OF DIRT ON HER MANTELPIECE, WITH HAND-LETTERED CARDS EXPLAINING WHERE THEY WERE FROM, SO'S ANYBODY WHO GAVE A TOSS WOULD KNOW ABOUT ALL THE WONDERFUL PLACES SHE'D VISITED.

NOW, I WAS IN A PLACE ONE TIME, SHE POPS IN ME HEAD. I'M NOT MUCH FOR SOUVENIRS, BUT THIS?

YOU CAN'T BE *SERIOUS*--

--WELL I'M NOT *JOKIN'*. SO WHAT'S THAT MAKE ME?

*CRAZY.*

LIKE A *FOX* IN A *HEN HOUSE.* AND I'VE GOT THAT *COCK'S HEAD* ON THE CHOPPING BLOCK.

YOU DON'T HAVE *CHICKEN SHIT,* TURRO.

YOU COMING WITH ME?

WE *WON'T* GET A WARRANT.

THEN LET'S NOT WASTE YOUR JUDGE'S TIME...

...OR *MINE.*

THIS MAY SOUND *SELFISH* TO SOMEONE LIKE *YOU*, FATHER...

...BUT I WAS *HAPPY*. BLISSFULLY SO. FOR MAYBE THE FIRST TIME IN MY LIFE, I FELT *UNFETTERED*.

THAT MUST HAVE BEEN... FOREIGN...

...TO SOME- ONE LIKE *YOU*.

WHAT ARE YOU *SAYING?* THAT I'M A *MISERABLE BITCH?*

NO, S.W., I MEAN A MAN IN YOUR POSITION--

--ON *TOP* OF THE *WORLD?*

I SUPPOSE. YOU ARE A VERY WEALTHY, POWERFUL MAN. YOU'VE TOLD ME YOURSELF HOW *RESPONSIBLE*--

--WHAT COULD *YOU* POSSIBLY KNOW WHAT I'M *RESPONSIBLE* FOR?

MY PARENTS. THEY WERE *MURDERED* WHEN I WAS JUST A BOY.

I SAW IT HAPPEN. I SEE IT HAPPEN, *OVER* AND *OVER AGAIN,* EVERY *GODDAMN* DAY.

THAT'S WHAT ALL THESE *GHASTLY TRINKETS* ARE ABOUT, THEN?--

--FIGURE *ONE* MIGHT GIVE YOU AN IN TO THE *OTHER SIDE?*

DON' SHUT-UP ON ME NOW, LUV. YA JUS' BARED YOUR *SOUL*...

I...

...AM *NAKED,* AREN'T I?

WOULDN'T 'AVE YOU ANY OTHER WAY.

NOW, YOU CAN GET RID'A THE LOT OF THIS *RUBBISH*...

...AN' GET ME ME OWN *PEDESTAL.*

'CAUSE STANLEY? I'M THE *ONE* OBJECT...

...CAN GIVE YOU WHAT YOU *DESIRE* MOST.

WHEN HE TOLD ME WHAT HE WAS CAPABLE OF I BEGAN TO *SWEAT.*

HE SAID IT WASN'T ENOUGH. THAT I'D HAVE TO *BLEED* AS WELL.

I *KISSED* HIM.

"HE...*FETTERED ME.*"

229

AND I **BLED.**

I'D DONE **SO MANY TIMES** BEFORE.

YOU KNOW THERE ARE CULTURES, FATHER, THAT BELIEVE SUFFERING INTENSE PAIN CAN OPEN DOORS TO A HIGHER CONSCIOUSNESS?

OF COURSE YOU DO. YOU'RE **PART** OF ONE.

AM I?

CERTAINLY. WASN'T SELF-FLAGELLATION A RELIGIOUS **DISCIPLINE**--FEEL THE **PAIN** OF YOUR **CHRIST** TO KNOW HIM THAT MUCH **BETTER?**

THAT DOESN'T GO ON ANYMORE.

ASSUMING WHAT DOESN'T GO ON BEHIND CLOSED DOORS IS **IGNORANT,** FATHER.

SO LET ME ENLIGHTEN YOU.

OPEN A **DOOR...**

AND HE WALKED AWAY, LEAVING ME THERE WITH MY PARENTS.

MY DEMONS.

"I SCREAMED FOR FREDO, AND HE CAME RUNNING.

"AS HE RELEASED ME, HE ASKED WHAT HAD HAPPENED.

"I COULDN'T TELL HIM WHAT JOHN CONSTANTINE HAD DONE, OR WHERE HE WAS...

"...SO I TOLD A *LITTLE BIRD* INSTEAD.

"AND AS THE LITTLE BIRD FLEW OFF, I *KNEW* THAT THE LIAR'S FATE WAS *SEALED.*

"BECAUSE ONCE YOU TELL A LITTLE BIRD SOMETHING, WHY, THEY JUST *CAN'T* KEEP THEIR BEAKS *SHUT.*

"THAT'S HOW *DAMNING INFORMATION* IS SPREAD...

"...AS THE CROW FLIES,

"FROM ONE *BIRD BRAIN*...

I'M NOT *HAPPY*, FATHER... ...NOT IN THE *LEAST*.

I...HAD NO *CHOICE*, STANLEY.

*PLEASE*, I'M NOT REFERRING TO WHAT YOU *JUST DID*, YOU *SAD*, PATHETIC MAN...

...I'M TALKING ABOUT WHAT *I'VE* DONE. THE *DEEP HOLE* IN MY HEART WHICH I DUG *MYSELF*.

*TELL...* TELL ME WHAT YOU *DID*, STANLEY...

FOR *GOD'S SAKE*, JUST *TELL* ME.

*NO.* BUT I WILL TELL YOU FOR *MY SAKE*. EARLIER TONIGHT...

...I WENT *HUNTING--* ARMED WITH A *VICIOUS* ANIMAL...

...AND WITH *MYSELF* AS *BAIT*.

SEE, I WAS AFTER A *NEW* HEAD FOR MY TROPHY WALL. SURE, LIONS AND TIGERS AND BEARS-- OH MY!-- MAY BE *DANGEROUS*...

...BUT NEXT TO A *LIAR*, THEY'RE BARELY *PUPPIES*, *KITTENS* OR *TEDDIES*.

'ELLO, STANLEY...

...'OW YOU *HANGIN'*?

JOHN. YOU SHOULDN'T HAVE CROSSED ME.

WHAT YA *MEAN*? I *GAVE* YOU WHAT YOU *ALWAYS WANTED*...

...S'NOT MY FAULT, LUV, IT *WEREN'T* WHAT YOU *WISHED* IT'D BE.

RICHIE? WHAT *YOU* DOIN' HERE?...

JOHN CONSTANTINE.

...AN' YOU BETTER MIND THAT LOAD A' *HATE* YOU GOT HOLD OF.

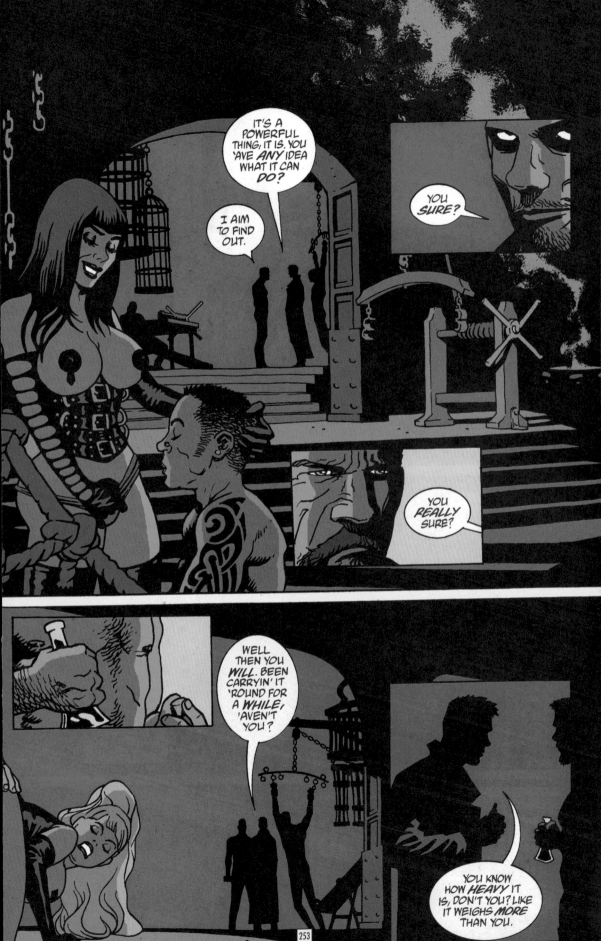

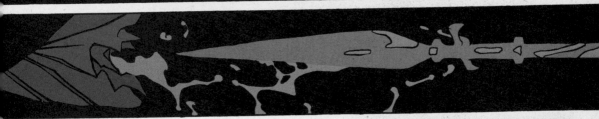

WHO ARE YOU?

JESUS FUCKIN' GOD...

REALLY? THOUGHT YOU WORE A *BEARD.* ANYWAY...

...WHERE WAS I? OH YES...

...ALONE.

CON...

...CONSTANTINE?

WHAT? YOU SEE HIM?

WHERE?

JOHN?

JOHN? WHY?

...WHAT'S HE DOING?

HE'S...

WHY'D YOU MAKE ME HATE YOU...

...WHEN I LOVED YOU?

MY HATE, IT DIED IN THE FLAMES. BUT MY LOVE...

...HE'S *CRYING.* REACHING OUT FOR YOU.

OH, JOHN, JOHN, JOHN... ...I'M SO *SORRY.*

SOOOO SORRY... YOU GAVE ME WHAT I *THOUGHT* I WANTED...

...AND I *MURDERED* YOU FOR IT. AND NOW, THE *KING* WHO HAS THE WORLD AT HIS *FINGER-TIPS...*

...CAN'T TOUCH WHAT HE DESIRES *MOST.*

FATHER...

...CAN *GOD* FORGIVE A *MAN...*

...WHO CAN'T FORGIVE *HIMSELF?*

C'MON NOW, FRANK, *UP* WITH YOU.

THE COMMISSIONER IS ON HIS WAY.

THAT IT, DETECTIVE?

DETECTIVE?

...

IS SOMEONE SMOKING?

END

# THE HELLBLAZER LIBRARY

Where horror, dark magic, and bad luck meet, John Constantine is never far away.

ALL TITLES ARE SUGGESTED FOR MATURE READERS

**ORIGINAL SINS**
JAMIE DELANO/VARIOUS

**DANGEROUS HABITS**
GARTH ENNIS/VARIOUS

**FEAR AND LOATHING**
GARTH ENNIS/STEVE DILLON

**TAINTED LOVE**
GARTH ENNIS/STEVE DILLON

**DAMNATION'S FLAME**
GARTH ENNIS/STEVE DILLON/
WILLIAM SIMPSON/PETER SNEJBJERG

**RAKE AT THE GATES OF HELL**
GARTH ENNIS/STEVE DILLON

**SON OF MAN**
GARTH ENNIS/JOHN HIGGINS

**HAUNTED**
WARREN ELLIS/JOHN HIGGINS

**HARD TIME**
BRIAN AZZARELLO/RICHARD CORBEN

**GOOD INTENTIONS**
BRIAN AZZARELLO/MARCELO FRUSIN

**FREEZES OVER**
BRIAN AZZARELLO/MARCELO FRUSIN/
GUY DAVIS/STEVE DILLON

**HIGHWATER**
BRIAN AZZARELLO/MARCELO FRUSIN/
GIUSEPPE CAMUNCOLI/CAMERON STEWART

Also from writer BRIAN AZZARELLO:

# THE 100 BULLETS LIBRARY

## WITH EDUARDO RISSO

With one special briefcase, Agent Graves gives you the chance to kill without retribution.
But what is the real price for this chance — and who is setting it?

ALL TITLES ARE SUGGESTED FOR MATURE READERS

**VOLUME 1:**
FIRST SHOT, LAST CALL

**VOLUME 2:**
SPLIT SECOND CHANCE

**VOLUME 3:**
HANG UP ON THE HANG LOW

**VOLUME 4:**
A FOREGONE TOMORROW

**VOLUME 5:**
THE COUNTERFIFTH DETECTIVE

**VOLUME 6:**
SIX FEET UNDER THE GUN

BROKEN CITY
RDO RISSO

**BATMAN/DEATHBLOW:**
AFTER THE FIRE

**JONNY DOUBLE**
with EDUARDO RISSO

**SGT. ROCK:**
AND A HA

# Look for these other VERTIGO books:

All VERTIGO titles are Suggested for Mature Readers

## AMERICAN CENTURY
Howard Chaykin/David Tischman/
Marc Laming/John Stokes

The 1950s were no picnic, but for a sharp operator like Harry Kraft opportunity still knocked all over the world — and usually brought trouble right through the door with it.

**Vol 1: SCARS & STRIPES**
**Vol 2: HOLLYWOOD BABYLON**

## ANIMAL MAN
Grant Morrison/Chas Truog/
Doug Hazlewood/various

A minor super-hero's consciousness is raised higher and higher until he becomes aware of his own fictitious nature in this revolutionary and existential series.

**Vol 1: ANIMAL MAN**
**Vol 2: ORIGIN OF THE SPECIES**
**Vol 3: DEUS EX MACHINA**

## THE BOOKS OF MAGIC
Neil Gaiman/various

A quartet of fallen mystics introduce the world of magic to young Tim Hunter, who is destined to become the world's most powerful magician.

## THE BOOKS OF MAGIC
John Ney Rieber/Peter Gross/various

The continuing trials and adventures of Tim Hunter, whose magical talents bring extra trouble and confusion to his adolescence.

**Vol 1: BINDINGS**
**Vol 2: SUMMONINGS**
**Vol 3: RECKONINGS**
**Vol 4: TRANSFORMATIONS**
**Vol 5: GIRL IN THE BOX**
**Vol 6: THE BURNING GIRL**
**Vol 7: DEATH AFTER DEATH**

## DEATH: AT DEATH'S DOOR
Jill Thompson

Part fanciful *manga* retelling of the acclaimed THE SANDMAN: SEASON OF MISTS and part original story of the party from Hell.

## DEATH: THE HIGH COST OF LIVING
Neil Gaiman/Chris Bachalo/
Mark Buckingham

One day every century, Death assumes mortal form to learn more about the lives she must take.

## DEATH: THE TIME OF YOUR LIFE
Neil Gaiman/Chris Bachalo/
Mark Buckingham/Mark Pennington

A young lesbian mother strikes a deal with Death for the life of her son in a story about fame, relationships, and rock and roll.

## FABLES
Bill Willingham/Mark Buckingham/
Lan Medina/Steve Leialoha/Craig Hamilton

The immortal characters of popular fairy tales have been driven from their homelands and now live hidden among us, trying to cope with life in 21st-century Manhattan.

**Vol 1: LEGENDS IN EXILE**
**Vol 2: ANIMAL FARM**
**Vol 3: STORYBOOK LOVE**

## THE INVISIBLES
Grant Morrison/various

The saga of a terrifying conspiracy and the resistance movement combating it — a secret underground of ultra-cool guerrilla cells trained in ontological and physical anarchy.

**Vol 1: SAY YOU WANT A REVOLUTION**
**Vol 2: APOCALIPSTICK**
**Vol 3: ENTROPY IN THE U.K.**
**Vol 4: BLOODY HELL IN AMERICA**
**Vol 5: COUNTING TO NONE**
**Vol 6: KISSING MR. QUIMPER**
**Vol 7: THE INVISIBLE KINGDOM**

## LUCIFER
Mike Carey/Peter Gross/Scott Hampton/
Chris Weston/Dean Ormston/various

Walking out of Hell (and out of the pages of THE SANDMAN), an ambitious Lucifer Morningstar creates a new cosmos modeled after his own image.

**Vol 1: DEVIL IN THE GATEWAY**
**Vol 2: CHILDREN AND MONSTERS**
**Vol 3: A DALLIANCE WITH THE DAMNED**
**Vol 4: THE DIVINE COMEDY**
**Vol 5: INFERNO**

## PREACHER
Garth Ennis/Steve Dillon/various

A modern American epic of life, death, God, love, and redemption — filled with sex, booze, and blood.

**Vol 1: GONE TO TEXAS**
**Vol 2: UNTIL THE END OF THE WORLD**
**Vol 3: PROUD AMERICANS**
**Vol 4: ANCIENT HISTORY**
**Vol 5: DIXIE FRIED**
**Vol 6: WAR IN THE SUN**
**Vol 7: SALVATION**
**Vol 8: ALL HELL'S A-COMING**
**Vol 9: ALAMO**

## THE SANDMAN
Neil Gaiman/various

One of the most acclaimed and celebrated comics titles ever published.

**Vol 1: PRELUDES & NOCTURNES**
**Vol 2: THE DOLL'S HOUSE**
**Vol 3: DREAM COUNTRY**
**Vol 4: SEASON OF MISTS**
**Vol 5: A GAME OF YOU**
**Vol 6: FABLES & REFLECTIONS**
**Vol 7: BRIEF LIVES**
**Vol 8: WORLDS' END**
**Vol 9: THE KINDLY ONES**
**Vol 10: THE WAKE**
**Vol 11: ENDLESS NIGHTS**

## THE SANDMAN: THE DREAM HUNTERS
Neil Gaiman/Yoshitaka Amano

Set in Japan and told in illustrated prose, this adult fairy tale featuring the Lord of Dreams is beautifully painted by legendary artist Yoshitaka Amano.

## THE SANDMAN: DUST COVERS —
## THE COLLECTED SANDMAN COVERS
1989-1997
Dave McKean/Neil Gaiman

A complete portfolio of Dave McKean's celebrated SANDMAN cover art, together with commentary by McKean and Gaiman.

## THE SANDMAN COMPANION
Hy Bender

A dreamer's guide to THE SANDMAN, featuring artwork, essays, analysis, and interviews with Neil Gaiman and many of his collaborators.

## THE QUOTABLE SANDMAN
Neil Gaiman/various

A mini-hardcover of memorable quotes from THE SANDMAN accompanied by a host of renditions of Morpheus and the Endless.

## SWAMP THING: DARK GENESIS
Len Wein/Berni Wrightson

A gothic nightmare is brought to life with this horrifying yet poignant story of a man transformed into a monster.

## SWAMP THING
Alan Moore/Stephen Bissette/John Totleben/
Rick Veitch/various

The writer and the series that revolutionized comics — a masterpiece of lyrical fantasy.

**Vol 1: SAGA OF THE SWAMP THING**
**Vol 2: LOVE & DEATH**
**Vol 3: THE CURSE**
**Vol 4: A MURDER OF CROWS**
**Vol 5: EARTH TO EARTH**
**Vol 6: REUNION**

## TRANSMETROPOLITAN
Warren Ellis/Darick Robertson/various

An exuberant trip into a frenetic future, where outlaw journalist Spider Jerusalem battles hypocrisy, corruption, and sobriety.

**Vol 1: BACK ON THE STREET**
**Vol 2: LUST FOR LIFE**
**Vol 3: YEAR OF THE BASTARD**
**Vol 4: THE NEW SCUM**
**Vol 5: LONELY CITY**
**Vol 6: GOUGE AWAY**
**Vol 7: SPIDER'S THRASH**
**Vol 8: DIRGE**
**Vol 9: THE CURE**
**Vol 10: ONE MORE TIME**

## Y: THE LAST MAN
Brian K. Vaughan/Pia Guerra/
José Marzán, Jr.

An unexplained plague kills every male mammal on Earth — all except Yorick Brown and his pet monkey. Will he survive this new, emasculated world to discover what killed his fellow men?

**Vol 1: UNMANNED**
**Vol 2: CYCLES**
**Vol 3: ONE SMALL STEP**

# Look for these other VERTIGO books:

## All VERTIGO titles are Suggested for Mature Readers

**BARNUM!**
Howard Chaykin/David Tischman/
Niko Henrichon

**BIGG TIME**
Ty Templeton

**BLACK ORCHID**
Neil Gaiman/Dave McKean

**THE COWBOY WALLY SHOW**
Kyle Baker

**DEADENDERS:**
**STEALING THE SUN**
Ed Brubaker/Warren Pleece

**DESTINY: A CHRONICLE OF**
**DEATHS FORETOLD**
Alisa Kwitney/various

**THE DREAMING: THROUGH THE**
**GATES OF HORN & IVORY**
Caitlin R. Kiernan/Peter Hogan/
various

**ENIGMA**
Peter Milligan/Duncan Fegredo

**THE FILTH**
Grant Morrison/Chris Weston/Gary Erskine

**GODDESS**
Garth Ennis/Phil Winslade

**HEAVY LIQUID**
Paul Pope

**THE HOUSE ON THE BORDERLAND**
Simon Revelstroke/Richard Corben

**HOUSE OF SECRETS: FOUNDATION**
Steven T. Seagle/Teddy Kristiansen

**HOUSE OF SECRETS: FAÇADE**
Steven T. Seagle/Teddy Kristiansen

**HUMAN TARGET**
Peter Milligan/Edvin Biukovic

**HUMAN TARGET: FINAL CUT**
Peter Milligan/Javier Pulido

**HUMAN TARGET: STRIKE ZONES**
Peter Milligan/Javier Pulido

**I DIE AT MIDNIGHT**
Kyle Baker

**I, PAPARAZZI**
Pat McGreal/Stephen John Phillips/
Steven Parke

**IN THE SHADOW OF EDGAR**
**ALLAN POE**
Jonathon Scott Fuqua/
Stephen John Phillips/Steven Parke

**JONNY DOUBLE**
Brian Azzarello/Eduardo Risso

**KING DAVID**
Kyle Baker

**THE LITTLE ENDLESS STORYBOOK**
Jill Thompson

**THE LOSERS: ANTE UP**
Andy Diggle/Jock

**MICHAEL MOORCOCK'S**
**MULTIVERSE**
Michael Moorcock/Walter Simonson/
Mark Reeve

**MR. PUNCH**
Neil Gaiman/Dave McKean

**THE MYSTERY PLAY**
Grant Morrison/Jon J Muth

**THE NAMES OF MAGIC**
Dylan Horrocks/Richard Case

**NEIL GAIMAN & CHARLES VESS' STARDUST**
Neil Gaiman/Charles Vess

**NEIL GAIMAN'S MIDNIGHT DAYS**
Neil Gaiman/Matt Wagner/various

**NEVADA**
Steve Gerber/Phil Winslade/
Steve Leialoha

**ORBITER**
Warren Ellis/Colleen Doran

**PREACHER: DEAD OR ALIVE**
**(THE COLLECTED COVERS)**
Glenn Fabry

**PRIDE & JOY**
Garth Ennis/John Higgins

**PROPOSITION PLAYER**
Bill Willingham/Paul Guinan/Ron Randall

**SANDMAN MYSTERY THEATRE:**
**THE TARANTULA**
Matt Wagner/Guy Davis

**THE SANDMAN PRESENTS:**
**THE FURIES**
Mike Carey/John Bolton

**THE SANDMAN PRESENTS:**
**TALLER TALES**
Bill Willingham/various

**SCENE OF THE CRIME:**
**A LITTLE PIECE OF GOODNIGHT**
Ed Brubaker/Michael Lark/
Sean Phillips

**SHADE, THE CHANGING MAN:**
**THE AMERICAN SCREAM**
Peter Milligan/Chris Bachalo

**SKREEMER**
Peter Milligan/Brett Ewins/Steve Dillon

**THE SYSTEM**
Peter Kuper

**TELL ME, DARK**
Karl Wagner/John Ney Rieber/
Kent Williams

**TERMINAL CITY**
Dean Motter/Michael Lark

**TRUE FAITH**
Garth Ennis/Warren Pleece

**UNCLE SAM**
Steve Darnall/Alex Ross

**UNDERCOVER GENIE**
Kyle Baker

**UNKNOWN SOLDIER**
Garth Ennis/Kilian Plunkett

**V FOR VENDETTA**
Alan Moore/David Lloyd

**VAMPS**
Elaine Lee/Will Simpson

**VEILS**
Pat McGreal/Stephen John Phillips/
José Villarrubia

**WHY I HATE SATURN**
Kyle Baker

**WITCHCRAFT**
James Robinson/Peter Snejbjerg/
Michael Zulli/various

**THE WITCHING HOUR**
Jeph Loeb/Chris Bachalo/
Art Thibert

**YOU ARE HERE**
Kyle Baker

Visit us at www.vertigocomics.com for more information on these and many other titles from VERTIGO and DC Comics
or call 1-800-COMIC BOOK for the nearest comics specialty store or go to your local book store